Chinatown Beat

Chinatown Beat

Henry Chang

Published by
Soho Press, Inc.
853 Broadway
New York, NY 10003

Library of Congress Cataloging-in-Publication Data

Chang, Henry, 1951-
Chinatown beat / Henry Chang.
p. cm.
ISBN 978-1-56947-478-5
1. Chinatown (New York, N.Y.)—Fiction. I Title.

PS3553.H34895C46 2006
813'.6—dc22   2006044284

10 9 8 7 6 5 4 3 2 1

For Dad, who followed his hopes and his sojourners'
dreams to America, and for Lucas, my son, the unseen shadow.
Chinatown will always be a place in our hearts.

Acknowledgments

Soulful thanks to Frances Chung for the inspiration, and to Frank Chin for blazing the way. Deep kowtowing gratitude to Doris Chong, for proving that Destiny is the shadow that precedes us all, and to Dana and Alfredo, for keeping the faith. Much love to my Chinatown brothers, my *hingdaai*, for riding shotgun through the years. They know who they are. And for Shemy Ayon, *esposa y amiga*, love and respect for always hanging tough.

Chinatown Beat

Nightrider

Johnny Wong pulled the black Lincoln over, onto the sidewalk halfway down the narrow street, territory of the Hip Chings. It was nine in the evening and before he could kill the engine they appeared, the stocky mustached man they called Uncle Four and the fragile Hong Kong lady, Mona. They were in the car before he could get out and open the door, the man motioning to him with a jerk of his hand.

"Lotus Blossom Club," said Uncle Four. The lady was silent as Johnny drove off wondering about her, passing through the nine neon-lit blocks in the rainy Chinatown night.

Uncle Four never said another word until they arrived.

"Come back eleven," he said. Mona followed him out, then down into the karaoke nightclub, never glancing back. When they were out of view, Johnny slammed the steering wheel hard, pausing for a long moment before urging the car away.

"*Dew nei louh mou hei,*" he hissed, *motherfucker,* and soon enough the chopping sound of windshield wipers brought him around to East Broadway, the lower part of town where the radio-car boys gathered and gossiped away the dead ends of their evenings.

They ate, slept, *breathed* Chinese, these expatriates, and they watched Chinese movies, shopped Chinese supermarkets, got laid in Chinese rub joints.

The laundromat attendant, the bank cashier, the locksmith, the mailman: all spoke Chinese.

The vocabulary of the car boys was limited; every other Chinese phrase rang out *motherfucker this, motherfucker that.* Whenever they did speak English it was sprinkled in between Chinese sentences, words that sang out: *focking got dem,* and a lot of *cok sooka, molla focka.*

Johnny felt superior but comfortable among them. He enjoyed their camaraderie, the spirit they generously shared with him. But he wasn't like them, and he knew it. They drove their limos because it was an easy enough life to fall into, and they found satisfaction in being their own bosses.

The Taxi and Limousine Commission dealt out franchises for seven thousand dollars, which included the radio hookup and the gypsy plates. Another five hundred dollars for the diamond sticker that allowed them to make pickups from the street. Lease or buy a black sedan. His used Continental had cost ten thousand. A 1990 model. It had eighty thousand miles when he bought it off Jung *gor,* brother Jung, who got cancer and went to San Francisco to die.

Johnny had labored three hard years for Big Wong's Construction and Design. Two years as *kup yee,* the steam presser, in the Rich Fortune sweatshop. Slaving. Saving cash.

All of it went into the car.

The other night drivers had refused to wait tables for long hours, sucking up to the white tourists. They disdained the misery of the market workers and the hard labor of the construction cowboy gangs, choosing instead to gamble and borrow, cheat and steal from their extended families. Their destinations were the racetracks and the gaming parlors, karaoke clubs and airport bars, nightclubs and whorehouses, glamorous places and secret hideaways where they chauffeured their shady clients of the night.

They were satisfied with themselves, and scoffed at Johnny's few foreign phrases. What the *fock* did they need the *gwailo*—white devil—English for?

The oldest driver was Gee Mun, sixty-three, a retired steam presser from the Rich Fortune. When he couldn't survive on Social Security alone, he became the off-driver whenever Johnny slept, which was mostly during the day. For the use of the car, Gee Mun gave Johnny twenty-five percent of his weekly tally. And he kept the Continental's tank full.

Including the pickups from the street and tips, Johnny was clearing eight hundred a week. Forty thousand a year. Not bad for an ex-Hong Kong waiter with no book smarts, and only fragments of English.

America had taught him to be cunning. With a little luck he figured to double the forty thousand in a year. The tips were always better at night, bigger *chaan jee*—cash—from men who gambled with their lives. But Johnny looked beyond jockeying the radio car. He believed he was going to make his money and get out, sell the car, invest his cash in other directions. Find a partner, someone with money and connections. A takeout counter in Brooklyn, go in with the Lucky Valley's third chef. The thirty-minute photo shop idea. The hardware store, the coin laundromat, the produce market. The fish market with the Chow brothers. A bakery franchise. Dreams bantered back and forth among the drivers waiting for calls from the night, in their dark cars.

"*Wong Jai*," they called Johnny, Kid Wong. "What's with this piece of pussy you keep talking about?" they asked. Johnny never elaborated, but he couldn't keep Mona out of his mind. The others knew this and teased him, knowing he'd only clam up, change the subject.

"*Ho sai li*," Gee Mun said, *dangerous*. The drivers knew why.

Women were sly, manipulative creatures by nature, instinctively so because of the weakness of their bodies.

Almost four months now he'd been driving her, since the end of the fierce New York City winter, a petite woman with deep black hair cut in a short bob. Always wore black. High heels. She had oval eyes with a translucent brown luster, set in a face of porcelain skin that threatened to shatter in the cold the only time he ever saw her in daylight. Her lips, cherry-blossom red.

It was a private contract. He kept her off the radio so none of the other drivers or dispatchers would know about her. But since he filled the bulk of his prime workday with sporadic pickups, leasing his daylight downtime to Gee Mun, the other drivers all knew he was doing side jobs. One of them had spotted Mona exiting Johnny's Continental, and word had gotten around, though nobody was sure who she was. Johnny became more careful about the routes he used.

"Secrecy," she'd said, was the key. He'd be required to keep her identity secret, to not talk about her. Johnny had agreed. "*Confidential*," she'd said, with an edge to her Hong Kong Cantonese.

The old man was short, maybe five-five, and stocky. He had a trim mustache, was balding on top and wore large jade rings on his meaty fingers. Everybody knew he was a big shot of the Hip Chings.

Now she was a regular four nights a week, three or four stops a night. The old man always gave the orders, but it was Mona who paid Johnny, cash. Three hundred a week. They hardly spoke the first two months, and never in front of Uncle Four.

Gradually she opened up to him, and now he wished she hadn't. The money and tips were good, but he didn't like to get involved with the customers, and what she'd confided in him was like a throbbing in his brain, a dull and bothersome headache.

The month before, after they'd begun to speak regularly, she gave him a fearful look and quietly said some nasty things about Uncle Four. He wished he hadn't heard it, wished he could do something about it, but knew it was impossible.

She said Uncle Four beat her and raped her, that he did this regularly. What the fock, he thought, she's his mistress. What the fock does she expect? Why stay with him then?

When he asked her why she didn't simply leave, she just cried. They didn't speak for a week after that, but he knew that she had given him part of her pain, and he was suffering along with her. She didn't have to speak. He saw it in her eyes every time they stole glances at each other, every time she touched his hand, every time she walked away behind the Mustache, never glancing back.

"Focken bitches," the other drivers said, "play you for a sooka."

"Don't let them use you," they warned.

"Money talks, bullshit walks. That's what those *hei* cunts care about."

Johnny was trying to control the fever slowly warming in his brain. He had two hours before he had to pick her up, until he had to face her eyes asking a hundred questions. He glanced at his wristwatch, tossed his bet money into the pool with the other drivers'. Two hours. He invested forty dollars at Yonkers Raceway. Snappin Dragon in the fourth. Samurai Warrior in the eleventh. What the hell, he thought, and closed his eyes.

But eleven o'clock came around faster than he expected.

The tears welled up quickly in her sloe eyes.

"Men have hurt me tonight, again," Mona whispered.

Johnny stood quietly and wrapped his arms around her until there were no more words. That's how it was with Mona. Her words came infrequently, calculated, wrapped in precise phrases full of poignancy and passion, but it was the heartbreak in her face, the tears spilling from her eyes, the quiver of her lips, the shiver of her body when he pulled her close, for him *that* was her true expression.

There was no escape from these images, Johnny knew. They wrenched his heart, and shredded his toughness. She was making him as vulnerable as he thought she was, and then, the other drivers laughingly warned him, she'd nail him.

He couldn't say no to anything she desired.

Later, when they lay together in his tenement flat, there was no need for the words he didn't have, the only sounds coming from the slap and pull of their bodies against each other, the soft clutching groans and whispers leading to hard, fast breathing and the sharp anguished cry of desperate pleasure.

Undercovers

Jack Yu leaned back from his desk in the empty squad room, tilted his head and rolled his neck over his bunched shoulders. He heard the ligaments pop, took a deep breath. There was a rotted wood smell from inside the floorboards that floated out every time it rained. He'd noticed it when he transferred precincts in July, during a week of summer storms. Now the rain that should have come in August arrived in October, cooling down Indian Summer, giving weight to the soggy leaves that blew into piles in the neighborhood parks.

The Fifth Precinct stationhouse, the 0-Five, was the oldest in the city, a four-story Federalist walk-up made of red brick, fronted by matching lanterns of Kelly green. The lanterns glowed in the mist, and rain dripped from the scrollwork around numerals that ran across the top of the building: 1881.

The blue-and-whites parked out front, up and down Elizabeth Alley, and out to Canal Street. Scooters. Vans. Undercover Dodges.

Jack could see them from the squad-room window, rolling out. The night patrols. He checked his watch. It was after ten, at the end of a long week full of bad dreams and sleepless fatigue. He knew he should go home. He had the weekend off and much to do.

He scanned the room, a shabby array of cluttered metal desks bumped up against each other across the creaky wooden floor. There was a color computer monitor but under the light from the dirty fluorescent overheads everything else was gray, worn. A bank of small steel lockers the detectives used. The surplus secretarial chairs. Across the long wall opposite him, sheets of assignment data and faded Wanted posters, covering like wallpaper anything that wasn't cracked and peeling.

He stroked the thin line of scar tissue that ran across his left brow, a nervous tic. His mind was drifting elsewhere and he clicked off the cheap fluorescent desk lamp, pushed back from the tangle of paperwork and open-case files. He ran his trigger fingers in tight circles around his temples and closed his eyes.

Running Dogs

Of the twenty-eight thousand, eight hundred and sixty-nine officers in the New York City Police Department, Jack Yu was the eighty-eighth cop of Chinese-American heritage. A lucky number, he once thought. At a sinewy five-foot-ten, he'd have failed the height requirement of a decade earlier. Now, four years into his career, he'd been transferred to Chinatown, back into his old neighborhood, a detective second grade.

After four months here he realized that working in the 0-Five was like living in two worlds at the same time. In a precinct that was ninety-nine percent yellow, the Commanding Officer was named Salvatore Marino, and the beat cops were ninety-nine percent white. The white cops put in their shifts, then beat a quick retreat back to the welcome of white enclaves beyond the colored reaches of the inner city. Chinatown was like a foreign port to them, full of experiences confounding to the average Caucasian mind. *Don't worry about it, Jake, it's Chinatown.* They were able to dismiss it as a troublesome nightmare, half-remembered and unfathomable. These Chinese were creatures unlike themselves, existing in a world where the English language and white culture carried little significance. Generations of sons and daughters of the Celestial Kingdom, they lived their lives by their own set of odd cultural rules. When a crime was committed, no one ever saw or heard anything. When the cops rousted them, it was a Chinese fire drill.

But Jack had grown up in Chinatown, knew what it felt like to look and breathe Chinese, to savor *foo yee, ga lei,* pungent and spicy aromas that white precinct cops wrinkled up their noses at, to speak and decipher regional dialects that sounded to the others like a back-alley cockfight.

He could remember a boyhood time when there were no Chinese cops, no Asian Squad, no interpreters, no community liaison, only *gwai lo* white devil faces in the blue uniforms howling *watseemotta no speakee Englee?*

Four months after his transfer, his father passed away in the Chinatown tenement Jack remembered growing up in. Realizing Jack was a cop, the landlord graciously allowed him the full month to clear out his father's belongings, purposely—Jack figured—never once mentioning the key money he'd taken from the old man those many long years ago.

When he opened his eyes, nothing had changed except the sound of the rain falling harder outside. Now, with his father six days in the still-soft ground of Evergreen Hills, he was feeling the tiredness heavy in his bones, the *fung sup*, arthritis, setting in. He adjusted the Detective Special nestled in the small of his back, then rose from the desk and took a black canvas knapsack from the steel lockers, checked it for disposable cameras, a pager, cellular phone, a silver flask. He went down the hundred-year-old stairs, exited onto Elizabeth Alley and followed the streets back to the Mott Street tenement he'd grown up in.

Dogs

The rain came down in thick sheets, rattled the stairwell windows as Jack climbed with leaden legs the five flights of tenement squalor.

Pa had lived here, all his forty-nine years of Chinatown life. A dead dog, the Chinese numbers meant: forty-nine, *say gow*.

Time and again Jack had asked Pa to move. Uptown. Crosstown. Queens maybe. A decent apartment they could rent somewhere, where the winter freeze didn't sneak in through the windows, where the dank misery of changing seasons didn't settle on the bedcovers. Where vermin didn't feast on the kitchen table, in the toilet, under the pillow.

Pa wouldn't hear of it, angry each time Jack brought it up. Where would he get his Chinese vegetables? His Chinese newspapers? Where would he find his cronies to gossip with, to keep track of who died, who lost at the track? All the important things. Didn't matter, Jack would say. There were *three* Chinatowns now. Sunset Park. Or Flushing.

Flushing, too far, would be Pa's answer. And Brooklyn, too many *hak yun*—blacks.

New frontiers were opening up for old-timers stuck too long, for newcomers too long locked out. No longer was the Chinese community defined by a single geographic boundary, but by a single consciousness of race. Not that any of that had mattered to Jack. He *knew* who he was, but knew he needed another space to live in, to be free from the burden his past here placed on him. But they trapped themselves, the old bachelors, wrapping themselves in their fierce Chineseness, taking pride in their disdain for American ways. Jack's ways. The man accusing the boy of trying to be white. Father and son were at cross-cultural odds, their lives a clash.

The keys were old and tarnished, the metal edges worn smooth and rounded from a hundred thousand turns. The lock itself was older than the keys, older than the grime in the hallway.

Jack twisted the key and heard the bolt open silently, effortlessly. He pushed open the creaking door and stepped inside Pa's world, his own past.

Nothing had changed. He wondered why he had ever thought it might have. Under the dim lifeless circle of fluorescent light spreading along the flaking gray ceiling, everything looked the same.

He stared at the scuffed and dented linoleum floor, produced the slim silver flask he'd prepared for the visit to the cemetery, full of the whiskey with which they'd celebrated life and mourned death. *Sanctified liquor.* He took a deep swallow, swinging his black knapsack down to the floor.

There was the tear-off wall calendar from the Hang Seng Bank, bright red with raised gold Chinese characters, trumpeting the Year of the Dog, the thin sheet of white paper printed with the number Four in black, freezing the day Pa died.

September 4, 1994, *gow say gow say,* twice a dead dog.

He crossed the stillness of the room to Pa's bed, pulled plastic packets of photographs from the bedside table, saw they were thick with dust except for spots where fingerprints had touched down recently, pushing across clear lines in search of memories.

How soon near the end do we begin to grope for our past?

When he opened the albums, the fingerprints led him to streaked and faded black-and-white photographs of himself as a child, then pictures of Ma, sometime in the 1940s. Her hair was shiny and combed back, away from eyebrows perfectly curved and sharp as a razor, her mouth slightly opened and dark lips smiling, revealing teeth framed in gold. She couldn't have been more than nineteen, an arranged bride, her almond eyes small lights of hope, resignation.

And there was the picture of himself with Pa, taken on a visit to the Tofu King almost a decade ago, by the front counter with the bean curd—*dao foo*—and the flat sheets of white noodles.

He swallowed quickly, noticed Pa's gourd-shaped bottle of *mao-tai* liquor on the floor. The seal had been broken but it felt more than half full. His mind drifted backward.

Jack was never the good son, but he struggled to maintain the truncated sense of family he had with Pa, who, in the few hours he was home from the laundry or the restaurant, was full of criticism or complaint, the smell of whiskey tinging his words.

Other times, around holidays, Pa was more melancholy, but managed a smile and brought home sweet cakes and fruit for his son, the *jook sing,* the American-born, the empty piece of bamboo.

Jack flipped the cellophane-covered pages, came across old

prints of Pa in the laundry, with Grandpa, who had gone back to China, beside him.

He took another swallow, then sliding his fingers through the dust-covered pages, came to a curled print of himself, in the poolroom, in between Tat Louie and Wing Lee, all mugging for the camera.

Now, sitting on his father's crumpled bed, Jack was unable to find the peace of mind he needed. What bothered him wasn't the neon lights from the Lee Luck restaurant sign whose colors intruded into the darkened room. It wasn't the clawing sound of rat feet scratching for entry somewhere along the baseboards, near the radiators. And it wasn't the smells of *lop cheung*—pork sausage—and *hom yee*—salted fish—long since leached into the walls, becoming one with the cracked and peeling green paint after thirty years, making time stand still.

It was the sense of being here, too late, the son, the cop. After the fact.

Somewhere down the stairs, across the hall, he could hear the vague singsong of Chinese opera, and closer, the rat-a-tat-tat action of Hong Kong videotapes.

He hadn't had the chance to say goodbye.

Decades of Chinese smell and sound hung so thick he could almost touch them, settling upon him a strong feeling of his father's presence. It wasn't Jack sitting on the bed after all. It was his sense of his father mixed with the spirit of his own younger self, surrounded by the ghosts of his father's bachelor apartment.

Jack felt thirst grabbing in his throat and emptied the flask. Pulling the few much-fingered pictures from the album, he slipped them inside his vest pocket and tossed the rest into the empty Seagram's carton on the floor.

* * *

As he lay down on Pa's pillow, memories came flooding; then the alcohol reached his brain and rolled him back a decade and four years, into a nightmare.

The three of them, Tat, Wing, and himself, racing across rooftops, leaping the spaces between buildings. Tat is throwing stones at windows as they run, three teenagers shrieking with juvenile laughter, curses following them from inside the tenement apartments.

They are clambering down a fire escape, dropping to a courtyard below.

Wing is shouting, "Race! Last one out sucks *lop cheung.*"

They are sprinting through a back alley, jumping cinderblock partitions, dashing for a connecting tunnel. The other end of the tunnel leads out to a side street, and they don't see the gang of Wah Yings until Wing crashes headlong into the leader.

He cuffs Wing with a backhand punch, snatches a gold chain from his neck. Wing lunges for the chain and the nasty boys break out their knives. They're flipping the chain from one to another, taunting Wing. Tat steps sideways, launches a side kick into the leader's groin, and suddenly everybody's screaming, cursing.

The Ying leader swings his switchblade around, and with a short punch blunts Wing's desperate charge. Wing lurches back, then charges again, his eyes white now.

There is a crash of black and white across Jack's forehead, blood from the gash running into his eye, as he watches Wing dropped by a chopping right hand, the color of red wine suddenly spreading across Wing's white T-shirt. Tat is screaming, and the Yings are beating the shit out of him.

Then everything is black, filled with the wails of a family overcome with grief. Racks of flowers fail to brighten a room cloaked in the choking odor of incense and death.

Wing is laid out in the casket and mourners are bowing, bowing, bowing, and burning death money. Tat is speechless and Jack watches him flee the funeral parlor as Wing's mother explodes with grief.

The sound of gunfire awoke him, yelling and shooting in the connecting back alley that led out to Mott Street. In the dark of Pa's apartment he could not tell what time it was, only that it was still black outside. More gunshots and screaming. He groped for his Colt Special, found it, and crept out onto the stairwell landing.

From the hallway window, he could see shadows and figures darting through the alleyway. He slapped out the hallway bulb with the gun barrel, crouched to observe the action below. But in another instant, it was quiet again. When he climbed down the fire escape into the alleyway, they were all gone, only a few spent shell casings on the ground and the burnt smell of gunpowder in the dark air. No bodies, and too dark to see if there had been bloodshed. He tried to shake the grogginess from his head, his adrenaline rush subsiding now, leaving a ferric taste in his mouth.

Back in Pa's apartment he sat upright on the bed and closed his eyes. Sleep didn't return and he reached for the flask and tilted it, but it barely wet his lips now. He picked up the gourd, shook it, refilled the flask with mao-tai. Then he found the keys to his Fury and went back out into the deadness of night.

The City

The streets were wet, black.

The midnight-blue Dodge Fury sat on the corner of Mott and

Bayard, a police permit on the dash visible through the windshield. No one was on the street when Jack slipped inside, started it up, let it idle while he fired up a cigarette, letting it burn halfway down before he slowly pulled away from the sidewalk, heading toward the East Side.

He rolled through the extended communities of Fukienese, Malaysians, Chiu Chaos, settlements stretching east to Essex and north to Delancey, into areas longtime Hassidic, Puerto Rican.

Whenever he cruised the neighborhoods, he thought of the boyhood Tat and Wing and he had shared. They were working-class Chinatown boys, but they were also Manhattan boys, who stayed mostly in the borough and came of age trolling through the various ethnic neighborhoods: Little Italy, the Village, Soho, Tribeca, Chelsea. When they ventured into Brooklyn or Queens, it was usually on the *snake* that roared through the subway tunnel, always a dusty noisy death march to get anywhere.

He used to like cruising the old places, remembering the year Tat got a used Volkswagen and they bombed around town, wolfing at girls.

Manhattan was twenty-two square miles and if he took his time, he'd cover it in two hours. He needed the air, needed to clear the alcohol from his head. The perspective from the driver's seat was a bittersweet pleasure to him.

He continued east.

The Greater Chinatown Dream, the Nationalists had called it: an all-yellow district in lower Manhattan running from the Battery to Fourteenth street, river to river, east to west, by the year 2000.

Then he turned the car north and made all the green lights through *loisaida*, the Lower East Side, past the Welfare Projects—the Wagner, Rutgers, Baruch, Gouverneur—federally subsidized highrises, which ran along the East River, blocs of buildings that stood out like racial fortresses. Blacks in the Smith Houses, Latinos in the Towers.

That's how the Lower East Side really was, not a melting pot but a patchwork quilt of different communities of people coexisting, sometimes with great difficulty.

Manhattan was symbolic of the rest of Gotham, the Big City, where the best walked the streets alongside the worst.

When the red light caught him, he was already past Alphabet City, in that part of the East Village where the druggie nation came to score: smoke, crack, rocks, pharmaceuticals, and a brand of Mott Street H tagged China Cat, so potent and poisonous it had sent twelve of the hardcore straight to junkie heaven in August, keeping the Ninth Precinct narcs tossing.

He powered down the window, kept the car headed north through Gramercy Park and Murray Hill, the wind buffeting his face, past the lights and shops of Midtown, the neighborhoods tonier now. He imagined the air was cleaner. Sutton Place. Beekman Place. The arriviste strongholds of the Upper East Side.

He drove through El Barrio, Spanish Harlem, the decay suddenly evident here, and crossed over above the Park at 110th, going west toward Morningside Heights and the enclave of Dominicans, a drug-dealing hub that connected New York, Connecticut, New Jersey. He paused on the Heights, long enough for another smoke, viewing the city spread out below him. The city was dying. *One murder every three hours. One rape every hour and a half. One robbery every four minutes. An aggravated assault every six minutes. A motor-vehicle theft every three minutes.*

There was a new governor and the death penalty was coming home.

The city was dying. He saw it every time he drove through the old neighborhoods. Saw it in the blacked-out windows of abandoned graffitied tenements, in sinking potholed streets and garbage-strewn parks. He felt it every time he heard the sirens of the patrols, the ambulances, the fire trucks, day and night, relentless. He heard it in the voices of the homeless, crying, begging, threatening. Death. It touched him every time he smelled the sewage on the waterfront, the choking urine stench of the subways. Old neighborhoods that had survived the World Wars and Depression years but could not survive crack and heroin.

Dope, he figured. Dope and despair feeding the death of the darkening city.

Farther south he slashed across the blackness of Harlem, the Thirtieth Precinct sitting in the valley where the island went flat, rose, and fell again, until he came to the highway.

It was only then, cruising back down along the Harlem River Drive, that the feeling caught up to him. He didn't know if what he felt was guilt, filling his soul with sadness, breaking through the hardness in his heart, the price of growing up an only child and without a mother's love. Perhaps, he thought, it was the finality of being alone, absolutely, without family now, after only a week, the Yu bloodline trapped, ending, with him. Perhaps, with Pa's passing, he was feeling his own mortality.

The lights across the river danced as he came south down the undulating highway, became misty as the tears flooded up behind his eyes. He blinked and the tears ran down the hotness of his cheeks, his breathing suddenly quick and heavy, a shuddering inside him.

He wiped a sleeve across his face, caught his breath as he turned on the dashboard radio, coming to the cutoff at Canal Street, the lights of Chinatown winking in the distance.

He twisted up the volume.

The rap anthem crashed out of the radio, violent and angry,

and he mashed the pedal to the metal, the Fury screeching up Canal the same way he was beginning to feel.

Freedom

The China Plaza was a modern elevator building, fifteen stories of beige and gray brick with lanai balconies, shoehorned in between turn-of-the-century Chinatown tenements and the foot of the Manhattan Bridge.

Apartment H was the only red door on the eighth floor, all the others painted a deep brown that suited the tan carpet and dark Taiwanese marble lining the corridor. Red was the color of luck, but behind the door the possessions of the old man were spread out to create the image of a private bordello.

The condo unit had a small living room with a closet bedroom stuck to it and a kitchenette squeezed into the corner. Positioned on the glass end tables and étagère shelves of the living room were assorted mini-pagodas, orange trees, dragon figurines and octagonal *bot kwa*, I Ching charms to fend off malevolent spirits and the breath of ill fortune. A small bowl of goldfish on a stand faced northeast, a red futon couch stood beneath the picture window, a double-happiness printed loveseat filled the remaining corner.

There was a smiling Buddha Kitchen God above the refrigerator, a lucky calendar behind the front door.

From the bedroom came the cadenced voice of Chinatown radio, the Wah Kue station reporting weather, time, news. A queen-sized bed filled the bedroom, covered with rose-colored sheets, the faint scent of Chanel on the pillows. Japanese *Vogue, Rendezvous,*

Hong Kong movie star magazines had fallen from the edge of the bed to the floor. A statuette of *Kuan Yin*, Goddess of Mercy, stood on the windowsill, just above the mirrored dresser covered with jewel-box chinoiserie. Draped on top of a leather ottoman was an Hermès scarf, vividly printed with Buddhist pilgrims, prayer wheels, a stupa, the heavenly Elements of the Universe. Prayers floating in the wind.

Mona, in silky yellow lingerie, stirred beneath the sheets, awoke, roused herself from the bed, moved like a cat across the bedroom, past the kitchenette, then parted the sliding red curtains at the balcony which looked out over Henry Street, eight flights above the noise of bridge trucks and the Kwik-Park garage below. She poured a rice bowl of water into the small pots of jade and evergreen plants that faced to the northwest: good *fung seui*, harmony with Nature. She had hoped that the various talismans, and her prayers to the Goddess of Mercy, could change her fate.

But her worst demon entered anyway. Uncle Four had the key, owned the apartment, came through the front door.

When she looked out on the street, she could see ghetto detritus on the blackened rooftops below, discarded mattresses and dismembered plastic dolls, tattered laundry drying across telephone wires. In the alleyways lay the carcasses of gutted refrigerators, air conditioners.

Once she saw a black man on top of a woman, doggy style.

The billboard above the China Plaza read:

LUXURY CONDOMINIUMS
VIEW OF RIVER, AND CHINATOWN.

It was early morning, a dead gray light. She brewed up a cup of *Ti-Kuan Yin*, Iron Goddess, spilled some ginseng into it, went over and sat in the red futon by the window. She closed her robe and stared ahead into the far distance, beyond the rooftops and the bridges, into the smog-colored sky.

Her fingers moved back and forth over a small jade charm clutched within her closed right hand, working it like a rosary. She contemplated freedom and death and the *tao,* the way of her life.

Jade Tao De Ching

The white jade octagon, a *bot kwa,* an I Ching talisman, was the size of a fat nickel. It nestled neatly in the soft of her palm, dangling from the flat gold Chanel bracelet on her wrist. She caressed it with the tip of her ring finger.

The jade was a translucent mutton-bone white, with a cool vitreous luster that in hard sunlight revealed tiny veins and serpentine, twisting fibers of a smoky-yellow hue. Not Shan, nor Chou, nor Ming dynasty. Quality jade, but not rare. Worthless compared to some of the pieces of jade Uncle Four had given her. But it had come from her mother, her only memento, and had touched three generations of the women of her family. It was her mother's soul.

On its flat sides, in bas-relief, were symbols of the Eight Trigrams. Yin and Yang together representing the Eight Elements of the Universe: Heaven, Earth, Wind, Fire, Water, Thunder, Mountain, Lake.

She dragged a red fingernail across one side. *Water over thunder. Not propitious to advance; wait and seek help.* In the center of the charm she felt the two embryonic snakes chasing each other's tail, forming the forever-changing symbol of the Yin-Yang, harmony of the cosmic breath.

She was able to read each symbol, Braille-like, in a single passing of her finger. Then she'd stack the Trigrams in her mind, forming Hexagrams, prophecies, from the *I Ching* or *Book of Changes.* Her fingernail slid down. *Heaven over Earth. Time of big loss, small gain. Untrustworthy people. Evil comes forth.* She flipped the charm, felt for the reverse symbols on the back side.

She felt weary.

Thunder over Earth. Oppression, chaos drains the spirit. Auspicious to appoint helpers. Preparation for action.

Her gaze came back into the apartment, into the faint light. She thumbed the remote toward the cable television, refreshed the Iron Goddess tea with the rest of the vial of ginseng, and saw the words *Black Cat* take shape from the snow on the screen. Maggie Kahn starring as the Female Assassin. The legend of Fa Mulan came to mind. If the woman warrior could ride into battle against a warlord army, surely she, Mona, could find the resolve to secure freedom from and vengeance against one corrupt old man. She sipped the brew and thought about recruiting help.

Johnny Wong

She knew the type, a young man with a hustler's good looks, always on the move. Waiting for the right *dai ga jeer,* big sister, to come along. She'd seen them plenty in TsimSha Cheui, working the disco circuit in the *soo-ga momie* pipeline. Uneducated youths working hard at pretending they were international playboys.

Despite the fact that she depended on them, Mona hated men, all men. They were mongrels, stray dogs, attack dogs, bloodhounds. Men wanted one thing only: her most precious part, her sex. They wanted to possess her for a short time, then discard her for someone younger. And there was always someone younger. Except for Johnny, the driver, who had asked for nothing and expected nothing, all the other men in her life had purchased her time, bought her body, played with her mind.

Nothing for nothing, that was the lesson she'd learned a lifetime ago, halfway around the world in Hong Kong, when at fourteen years of age, the Triads had forced her to sell her body to repay her father's gambling debts. When her mother found out, she cursed her husband, then immediately suffered a heart attack. Mona never forgot that extra week in the seedy brothel, on her back, to pay for the funeral.

Her mother's curse came true. In the end, they killed her father anyway, those evil men with snake tattoos and black hearts.

By the time Uncle Four came to Hong Kong, almost three years ago, Mona had been promoted to China City, the big nightclub on Kowloon where hundreds of *siu jeer*, young ladies, sold themselves while seeking overseas American Chinese with the promise of green cards. She and Uncle Four discovered they had roots in the same province in China, and that had served as convenient-enough excuse for her to follow him to New York City, overstay her visa, and disappear underground.

At first, all had gone well with this older man, at sixty, some thirty years her senior. Although he was married, Uncle Four provided her with the clean co-op apartment, food, fun money for clothes and personal expenses. In return she accompanied him only at night—twice, three times a week—a decoration on his arm that he liked to show off in the gambling houses and karaoke nightclubs.

All types of men ogled her wherever they went, raping her with their eyes as she passed, hungry-looking men who stared and didn't look away when she flashed her eyes at them. None of this went unnoticed by Uncle Four, but he gave big face to the club owners and didn't bring trouble to their places.

As time went by he accused Mona of looking back at some of the younger men, suspected her of harboring other desires, causing him big loss of face. This was unacceptable. He was, after all, an elder man of respect. Gradually he became abusive and violent, threatening her with deportation, even death, if she ever tried to leave him. As leader of the Hip Chings, who sponsored the Black Dragons, his people were everywhere and she feared she would never escape.

Jing denq, she cried secretly. It was destiny, her Fate.

Man-Devil

Out on the edge of the neighborhood, the river wind blew chill into the somber Chinatown day, and swirled dust devils around the beastman who stood on the street corner, watching the working-class families entering the Housing Projects.

He saw the child, grade-school bag in her small hand, with the old woman, grandmother, he figured, withered, bent, *useless.* When they entered the project elevator, he followed them into the urine stench, watched as the grafittied door slid shut behind them. After the child tapped the seven button, he pressed number sixteen, *lucky today.* The old woman glanced at him only briefly, saw a clean-cut Chinese and was reassured. The little girl's long black hair hung down her back, her eyes reached just above the buckle of his belt.

They came to the seventh floor. The door slid back and the old woman pushed out past the swinging door to the hallway. In one motion, he grabbed the little girl, shoved the grandmother onto the linoleum, slammed the door.

The girl froze, her jaw slack with fear.

The elevator reached Eight, one of his hands cupped over her mouth, the other feeling for the switchblade in his pocket. At Fifteen, he took her into the stairwell, her eyes big, wet now, too afraid to cry. She was half-dragged, half-carried, up the stairs, her whimpering unheard over the echoing thunder of his footsteps, the feeble screams of grandma far below now.

On the roof landing he showed the knife but spoke calmly in a dialect of Chinese she barely understood.

Um sai pa, he said, eyes freezing her, *don't be afraid.* She nodded her answer at the point of the blade. *Good,* he murmured in English, tugging down her underpants. *Seven, maybe eight years old,* his eyes swallowed her. He put his fingers on her, like ice. *Good, this country America,* as he unbuckled his belt . . .

Bones

Jack nosed the Fury into Evergreen Hills cemetery, parked it behind a line of mausoleums, and went to the plot in the Chinese section.

The empty cemetery looked pastoral as a brief patch of sun spread over the clipped grass, throwing long shadows across the rows of tombstones. It was cooler now as Jack kicked away the twigs of the dying season, gravesweeping beneath his father's tombstone. He planted a bouquet of flowers, produced his flask and toasted mao-tai to Father and earth. *Sorry, Pa,* he thought.

He lit sticks of incense, took another slug from the flask, then poured out a small stream making a wet circle in the dirt. When his thoughts tumbled into speech, *sorry* was all he could say, not for anything in particular, but for the general torment of unfulfilled dreams.

"Sorry," he repeated, bowed three times, planted the incense, and touched his fingers to the graceful cuts in the gray stone.

Sorry you never struck it rich.

Sorry I never struck it rich.

He moved the tin bucket over and torched various packages of death money for gambling in the house of the dead.

Sorry no big house in the South of China.

Sorry no farm with fish, and rice paddies.

Sorry no bones to return to Kwangtung province.

He fed the shopping bag of gold-colored paper taels into the fiery heap in the bucket. He stirred the flames with a branch, produced three packs of firecrackers.

Sorry we never had a car.

Sorry I didn't become a doctor or lawyer.

He tossed the fireworks into the flames, stepped back as the staccato explosions rocked the silent cemetery.

Sorry about moving out on you.

He tilted the flask and took another long hard hit. *Sorry, sorry, sorry.*

Big Uncle

As was his custom on Saturday mornings, Wah Yee Tom left the office of the Hip Ching Labor and Benevolent Association, met

Golo Chuk, the enforcer, and went down the block to the Joy Luck *dim sum* parlor where he held court for one hour at the large round table by the back wall.

During this hour, Wah Yee Tom dispensed charitable favors to members of the Association and their families, and mediated problems that arose within the ranks.

Wah Yee Tom, a.k.a. Uncle Four, was *advisor for life* to the Hip Ching tong, the number two tong in America, a bi-coastal organization with thousands of members, a multi-million-dollar bankroll, and an aging conservative leadership. The tong was the American offspring of the international Triads, Chinese secret societies whose roots reached back to warlords and dynasties preceding China's birth as a nation. The numerous Triads had supporters and agents in every Chinese community in the world.

A waiter brought Uncle Four's usual pot of *guk bo cha*, poured two cups and withdrew. Golo escorted some people into the restaurant and seated them by the takeout counter in the front. Then he went back to the round table, sat, and the two men sipped tea together before Uncle Four spoke.

"What do we have?" he asked quietly.

"A widow," Golo answered. "Needs money."

Uncle Four's eyes shifted to the disparate group at the front as Golo continued. "A member with a complaint, and a young guy who came off the ship that crashed the other night."

"Put him last," said Uncle Four.

The first matter at hand was a request for help from an elderly widow whose husband had been a longtime member before his death. The wrinkled old woman with gnarled hands had been beaten and her apartment had been ransacked by a gang of Puerto Rican beat girls during a push-in robbery in the housing projects. She was terrified and wanted to return to China to die but had no money, the *say loy sung neu,* nasty Latina girls, having taken everything.

Uncle Four spoke quietly to Golo, who rose and escorted the old woman to the door. He gave her a handful of hundred-dollar bills from a wad in his pocket, whispered in her ear, and patted her reassuringly across the shoulder. She nodded her head, almost *kowtowing,* before leaving the restaurant.

Golo returned to the table.

"She agrees," he said, "to provide us with the address and the keys to her apartment, along with the canceled rent checks and telephone bills of the year previous."

Uncle Four nodded, sipping thoughtfully from his cup of tea, thinking that he would instruct Golo to dispatch several Dragons to take over the apartment. It would become an additional stash- or safe-house, and the gang could distribute their Number Three *bak fun,* heroin, from there, to the low lifes and the animals.

The second person to entreat Uncle Four's help was pale for a Chinese; there was a sickly, pasty tone to his face. He wore a cheap jacket and tie over jeans and his black shoes were scuffed, slanted along the heels with wear. He wrung his hands and looked about nervously.

Golo brought him to the table, where he respectfully introduced himself as a new member who owned a small takeout counter down near Essex Street, at the edge of East Broadway. He'd paid his dues and posted the Hip Ching membership placard, but was still being shaken down by three rival crews, one of them being Dragons—a crew of young guns.

They'd threatened him and taken fifty dollars from his register.

Uncle Four knew the territory, a no-man's land picked over by rival gangs, the Fuk Chings, the Tong On. It was half a mile away from Pell and Division Streets, the heart of Dragon turf.

It was more difficult to manage the fringes of the empire, he thought, things were more desperate out there on the edge, the Fukienese refusing to respect truce and territory.

He gave the man a hundred dollars and assured him the problem would be *gau dim,* taken care of.

The man thanked him profusely and never took his eyes off Golo until he was out of the restaurant. Golo checked his watch, signaled the next young man over.

He was a skinny Fukienese with a scared look, and Golo conversed with him in Mandarin, calmed him, gave him a cigarette. He talked and Golo translated.

"His name is Li Jon. He walked off the highway, found a payphone. He called the number they gave him in China. When they called back, he gave them the words on the street signs. Half an hour later a black car picked him up and dropped him in Chinatown. He's been walking around town since."

Uncle Four blew the steam gently around the rim of the thick porcelain cup. "What about the ones who drowned?" he asked the Fukienese.

The man took a breath. His eyes went distant.

"It was the ocean, the darkness. We're not used to it, you see." He shivered, continuing, "We're from the South of China, the water is always warm. When we dropped in, the water was so icy my muscles were in shock. I stroked and kicked but went nowhere. I was afraid my bones would freeze and snap and I'd sink and drown. People were screaming. Less than a hundred yards to land, I could see it. It was hard to breathe. My hands were chopping at the waves. I thought my heart would explode. I started to swallow saltwater."

His eyes came back.

"Then a wave caught me and suddenly there was a short walkway of land, where it rose up under the water. I caught my breath and saw the beach again. There was more screaming far behind me, near the ship. More people drowning. Another minute I was ashore, changing my clothes. I found a phone, made the call. I'm here. They said the Big Uncle would have work for me."

Uncle Four lowered his teacup to the table, leveled a hard look at the Fuk Chou man.

"Young man, you have come a long way, and you owe a lot of money. Remember well the terror of the ocean if you ever consider reneging on your debt. Your punishment will be a hundred times worse. You cannot hide. We will find you. Or America will swallow you up. Your family back in the village, all are at risk for you. So work hard. Don't mix with the *gwai lo*. Repay your debt, *then* seek your fortune. Every man has a chance here. Do not fumble away your golden opportunity."

"Eternal thanks, Big Uncle," the young man said quietly.

Uncle Four nodded at Golo, who escorted the man out, dictating directions into his ear.

The restaurant began to fill for *yum cha* and Uncle Four took his tea to the big glass window and watched pedestrians passing along the shadowy narrow street. His thoughts drifted back a half-century, to when he had arrived in New York City as a Toishanese child. He'd grown up in a time when Chinese men faced off in back alleys with hatchets and cleavers. A time when the storied tongs had a death grip on the old sojourners.

More than forty years had passed since that night in the dusty room down in Mongkok, on the Kowloon side, with the ancestral scrolls and the flags of the mythical heroes on the wall, with twenty other *dog* recruits, where he drank the blood of a man and fowl mixed with wine, and swore on his life the Thirty-Six Oaths of secrecy and loyalty to his Triad blood brothers.

Now the Red Circle Triad had expanded outside of Communist mainland China, remaining a powerful force in Hong Kong, but spreading to Singapore, Amsterdam, Canada, and South America.

He remembered hand signals, instinctively ran his fingers along his forearm in an X, then hands, pitching fingers across his palm. *Two fingers, three, five,* dragon's head and tail. He grinned at the foolishness of his youth.

Uncle Four was not pleased about the way things had changed. The tongs were depicted as thuggish, evil organizations. The newer waves of immigrants didn't give respect to them. And every time business was transacted, there were the lawyers, the brokers, the city officials, the bank regulators. The paperwork, the documentation. He preferred things under the table. Quiet. Secretive.

Forty years ago, the Hip Chings had welcomed his return as a hero, never mentioning the jail time he'd served for what the white officials called *tax evasion and labor racketeering.* The tong had rewarded him a full share of the Chinese Numbers route he helped create before his incarceration. They had supported his family in China, where his first wife died, where elderly relatives were sustained into old age.

Uncle Four had taken the numbers proceeds from the hundred membership storefront operations and invested in the *bak fun* and in gambling basements from Pell Street to Division Street. Ten percent of the gross from gambling was paid back to the tong, blood cash that funded the benevolent work of the Association.

When the Feds investigated him, he dispersed his holdings and retired from the Association, becoming its advisor for life.

He sipped the tea thinking, *There is no respect anymore.*

Long shadows jagged along the street. He blew steam off the tea cup as the plastic wall-clock chimed, then waved goodbye to

Golo who was already on the street, lighting up his trademark 555. Uncle Four knew it was too early in the day for the gang boys, so Golo would probably wait until the afternoon races at OTB before taking up the matter with the *daai gor*—big brother—in charge. No big deal. He would make them see the foolishness of their young minds. The punks were attracting attention toward the Hip Ching and it was bad for business.

It wasn't like in Hong Kong, where he could thrash the little *dogs* inside the Triad assembly hall. Here, the Chinese gangs had their own membership of undisciplined teenaged hotheads, including many who didn't speak or read Chinese, controlled supposedly by their "elder brothers," the *dailo*.

Uncle Four shook his head disdainfully.

They had even had to translate the Thirty-Six Oaths into English, which came out to only twelve oaths, to simplify the ritual, as the street boys were incapable of memorizing thirty-six consecutive ideas.

Of the Twelve Oaths, even the most lethal sounded blunt, almost businesslike, in English reading: *I will obey the tong, and if I do not, I will die under the condition of being shot; the secret of the Association must be kept and if I do not do this I will be stabbed a thousand times; and if the tong comes into difficulty and I do not come to its aid, I will die by the electric shock, or be burned by fire.*

Uncle Four finished his tea, and stared out over his world with the same disappointment he was feeling toward the young gangsters. *No discipline these days,* he thought, as he left the Joy Luck, heading toward Confucius Towers, completely ignoring the shortness of his shadow that preceded him down the pavement.

Sex/crimes

He was an hour early for the four to midnight shift but he didn't want to leave the leftover incense and hell money in the Fury. Bad luck. Better to stash them in his locker.

Alone in the squad room, he felt abandoned somehow. It wasn't until he punched up the TV that he realized why there was the absence of uniformed officers. On screen was an overhead aerial helicopter view of protestors coming across the Brooklyn Bridge, the National Organization of Women, NOW, and a coalition of anti-war and anti-poverty protesters bearing the banners of gay and lesbian rights activists and workers' rights groups, were marching, more than a hundred thousand strong. Their route snaked past Chinatown to Seventh Avenue, then north to a rally at Madison Square Garden. The march siphoned off NYPD manpower from every precinct in Manhattan, leaving the 0-5 precinct understaffed. The TV commentator described the "left liberal agenda" supporting the Clinton Democratic administration. They were, he said, united for peace and justice.

Jack tossed the incense into his locker and was closing it when the desk phone jangled.

It was Paddy, the desk sergeant, downstairs.

"There's a man down here," he said, "who needs to speak to a Chinese."

"Where's the translator?" Jack asked.

"Chin's out on meal, and Wong took a personal day."

"Coming down," Jack said as he hung up the phone.

Sergeant Paddy, behind the desk, loomed over the man, who was watching Jack approach. He was Chinese, forty-something, dressed like he might be an office worker, shift manager, something like that.

"How can I help you?" Jack asked, his Cantonese sharp.

The man responded in Toishanese, the tongue of laundrymen and waiters.

"I would like to report that there has been a rape," he said guardedly. "But there are conditions . . ."—Jack's eyes narrowed—"that I need your help with."

Jack waited, then said, "Okay, what do you need?"

Paddy jerked his head toward the rear of the room. Jack walked the man slowly to the benches by the back stairs. After he was seated, the man said, "My niece was raped. She is ten years old. Her grandmother is beside herself—"

"Slow down," Jack said quietly, his Toishanese all slang now.

"Her father does not like the police. He does not want to report it. My sister, the mother, feels the shame of it will harm the girl further."

Jack was beginning to have a bad feeling about this.

"Not one of them will speak to a *gwailo* officer."

Sex Crimes Unit, Jack was thinking.

"I am hoping to convince them. To speak to you."

Jack took a breath, through his nose the way a boxer does when he's under pressure. "Come upstairs," he said.

In the empty room, Jack asked, "When did this happen?"

"This morning. About five hours ago."

There was a pause. Jack knew the victim should already have been examined, valuable time had been lost. He wasn't on the clock yet, but to see if this man's story was true, he was good to go.

Normally, a call would have come into the precinct and they would have processed it. Ms. Chin, the translator, would get involved if needed. Get the basic information from the complainant. A

uniformed officer would be dispatched to the scene and determine the facts, report back to the sergeant. They would notify
EMS, get the victim to a hospital, administer a rape kit test. The
detectives of the Sex Crimes Unit would be called to respond, *the
experts*, to determine the who's and why's. Ask the victim to iden-
tify photographs. Check local and state files for pedophile predators of the type involved. Track and locate. Surveillance if
necessary. Bring suspects in for questioning. Draw up timelines to
trace the crime back and forth. Check the prison population
based on the perpetrator's profile. Post composite sketches of the
suspect. Seek help from the local population. The news media,
TV, radio, and newspapers, could help.

The uncle's eyes went distant as he continued. "The grandmother and the little girl. They had gone to the supermarket. It
was around ten-thirty or eleven this morning. They were in the
elevator, coming home."

Jack was seeing it clearly in his mind.

"There was a man inside, riding up with them. I think he followed them in. On their floor they started to get off. But the man
pushed grandmother, *Ah Por*, down, and took the little girl to the
roof."

The uncle's jaw clenched. He swallowed, took a breath.

"The mother and the grandmother found her on a landing,
crying. Her underwear was missing. And she was bleeding.

The uncle's chest heaved, his hands clenched, his knuckles
turned white.

"What did he look like?" Jack asked.

"The grandmother said he was cleancut, that he wasn't an
older man, but not a kid either. Maybe twenty to thirty years old.
Chinese, it's hard to tell sometimes."

"What else?"

"The mother is concerned the girl may be pregnant."

"Is the family there now?"

"I will take you to them." He showed Jack a Con Edison bill with an address on it.

Jack went to the photo file cabinet, pulled all the pictures of Asian men involved in sex crimes. There were seven photos in all, men of apparently different ages, but possible perps. *Hard to tell with Asian men.* He picked up the phone and tapped up Paddy.

"Sarge," he said, "it's a possible rape. I'm going to need the Sex Crimes Unit."

"Forget about it," Paddy answered, "there's reports of Hispanic men attacking women protestors along the parade route. Snatching them near the Penn Yards. Sex Crimes is all tied up."

"I'm going with the man to the scene. I'll work up the information." He looked at the Con Ed bill. "It's 10 Catherine Slip. In the Smith Houses."

"I'll patch it along, but Sex Crimes won't be available until after the protest march."

Downstairs, Sergeant Paddy watched Jack and the man exit the stationhouse, both of them somber. Jack flashed him a hard look and shook his head as more uniformed officers trooped in.

The four to midnight shift was finally arriving.

Catherine Slip was six blocks off. Along the way, Jack stopped at Tong's Variety Toys and purchased a black-and-white panda bear, a prop he hoped would help put the victim at ease when he interviewed her.

The uncle appeared nervous, anxious, as they walked together.

"You're doing the right thing," Jack said. The uncle nodded, uncertainty in his eyes.

"Why?" Jack asked. "Why does the father dislike the police?"

The uncle shook his head, a look of disdain crossing his face.

"He was mugged by some *loy sung*, Spanish men. Over there somewhere. When the police came, he felt they did nothing. Another time, a policeman wrote him a traffic ticket. He couldn't speak enough English to argue. He felt he did nothing wrong. Just sitting in the car. It still cost him a hundred dollars."

They were approaching the fringe of the neighborhood.

The Smith Houses were brown brick buildings, each seventeen stories tall, a low-income housing development located in the bowels of the Lower East Side. They had been part of the post-war boom in public housing construction, stacking poor families, black, Latino, white, in isolated areas, families that lived off Welfare programs, generations growing up on WIC coupons, and food stamps. Subsistance on assistance.

Twelve buildings hunkered down next to the East River, by the Brooklyn Bridge and the South Street exit ramp of the FDR, beginning just a block away from the city's police headquarters.

Jack remembered schooldays, when he and Wing Lee came by the community center gymnasium, looking to play basketball, fearfully avoiding the black men who drank from quart bottles of Colt .45, pitched quarters against the gym wall, and rolled dice when they weren't selling bags of marijuana, coke, maybe heroin. Pa had told Jack not to go down there, to the *jingfu lau*—government housing projects—where every Chinese resident had been mugged at one time or another. One day that last summer, a group of black kids stole his basketball, and tore his Knicks T-shirt. He never went back. *Fond memories.*

Now, they were passing the white sign with red letters that read " Welcome to the Alfred E. Smith Houses."

Ten Catherine Slip was beyond the gymnasium, on the way to the East River. Long-haul trucks and black cars lay low under the ramp of the FDR. The main entrance to the building was along a deserted stretch of sidewalk, cracked and dropping down toward the river.

They stepped into the stench of junkie vomit, passing graffiti-covered walls. **NWA**, the rap group Niggers With Attitude, in big block marker. To the elevator. *Niggaz 4eva*.

Apartment 16 was located in the crook of the long corridor. The uncle knocked. There was the sound of the peephole sliding open behind the two-way glass. A moment, then the uncle said, "It's me."

The door opened into a small living room. A kitchenette, and bedrooms beyond. Plastic slipcovers on the couch and chairs. Aluminum foil on the wall above the oven and range. The smells of *hom yee*, salty fish and steamed rice.

The father was fortyish but gray already and thinning. The mother was red-eyed; she kept her left hand over her mouth. Jack could almost hear the heaviness of her breath. The grandmother peeping out from one of the bedrooms. The girl was inside.

" I'm *lo* Yu," Jack announced quietly, giving his surname, and family association by inference. He showed his badge to the father, looked to the uncle, then to the mother.

" I understand your daughter may have been injured?"

The mother gasped behind her hand. The uncle braced his sister.

"For your daughter's sake," Jack half-pleaded, "she needs medical attention. Also, the physical evidence will help us catch this *animal . . .*"

The father gave him a skeptical look. " The police have never been any help. They pick on us Chinese. I can get help my own way."

Jack took a step closer and said, "Sir, your daughter may be pregnant. This is our first concern." The mother averted her eyes at Jack's glance.

"Please help us," continued Jack. "This beast is out there, running free. He may yet attack another Chinese girl. You can help us put an end to this."

The father's mouth formed a sneer but he remained silent.

"No one else will know. The victim's identity will be kept confidential."

The victim. Victim. The word resonating in Jack's head. The mother began to cry, sobbing softly. Jack took a breath through his nose. The father was slowly relenting, realizing the limits of his options, Jack felt. He huddled with his wife, comforting her.

The uncle led Jack to the near bedroom. The lights were dim, and the grandmother was stroking the girl's back, the two of them seated on the bottom bed of the double-decker. The little girl looked away, distant.

Jack beckoned the grandmother to the hallway light and showed her the photographs from the perp file.

"Was it any of these men?" he asked.

She took maybe two minutes to view the seven photos.

"None of these," she said. "He was lean, with short hair. Like you."

"How tall?"

"About your height. Shorter, but not by much." *Five-foot-nine*, Jack noted.

"Eyeglassses?"

"No."

"Did you notice any scars? "

"No."

"A mustache?"

"No. He looked like a regular young man."

"Is there anything you remember clearly about him?"

She paused for a moment, looking toward his feet. "He had on thick black shoes. They were dirty. Like he worked in a *gung chong*, a factory, or a *chaan gwoon*, a restaurant."

As Jack jotted down the information, the girl appeared at the edge of the door, round sad eyes peering up at him. He smiled, taking the panda from his jacket.

"Hi," he said softly to her, showing her his gold badge. "I'm a policeman, and I brought a friend for you." He gave her the panda. The girl accepted it, looking down at the floor. Jack knelt, his eyes at her level.

"I'm going to punish the bad man who hurt you. But I'm going to need your help."

The girl hugged the bear. Through the bedroom window, Jack could see the afternoon darkening, the overcast day running toward its end.

"I'm going to take a walk with *ah por*—grandma. *Sook-sook*—uncle—will stay with you. When I come back I'm going to ask you some questions, okay?"

"Okay," the girl answered, her voice barely audible.

Speaks English, Jack noted as he turned toward the front door.

They took the stinking elevator up, then the hallway stairs, climbing the steps up to the landing, the old woman leading the way.

Grandmother pointed to where the girl had sat, bleeding, on the cement floor. She had feared her granddaughter was dead. In the waning light of the afternoon, Jack could see no visible clues, no articles of evidence left behind anywhere, only the stillness of the cinderblock enclosure. *Crime Scene Unit*. They might have the resources and the equipment to take it further. Sex Crimes Unit, maybe. *Break out the bloodlights, and all that high-tech gear.* . . But there was nothing here.

* * *

They were walking back down the graffiti-tagged stairwell, Jack keeping an eye out for evidence, when his radio blared. It was Sarge Paddy's voice over the static.

"SCU's down by you. They need to know what apartment."

"Sixteen," Jack barked, "apartment sixteen."

They stepped over the puddles of urine, past hypodermic needles and empty beer cans, until they reached their landing.

SCU came out of the elevator just as they approached the apartment, two white female undercover detectives, one more mannish than the other. Jack introduced himself, gave one his detective's card and handed over all the information he'd jotted down. The one with the short spiky haircut looked over the sheet of paper and complimented Jack on his thoroughness. Jack explained that he hadn't interviewed the victim yet, but believed the girl spoke English.

"We'll take it from here then," the taller one said. "Thanks for your help."

"Sounds like the same perp from the case in the 0-Six," the other added. "Another Chinese girl, about the same age. But this was in the projects on the West Side. The Varick Houses, near the Holland Tunnel."

"Can you get me some composite sketches?" Jack asked, showing interest. "Also a picture of the victim?"

"Be in your mailbox at the 0-Five," said the taller one. "First thing tomorrow."

"Thanks." Jack nodded. "I'll see what I can squeeze out of the neighborhood."

"That's a bet," she said, breaking a smile.

All together, they entered the apartment.

* * *

The father stepped forward, away from the mother who remained near the small kitchenette, and stood squarely in front of the white *gwai por*, women detectives.

"Don't be nervous," Jack warned him in a loud enough voice to command him to back off. "These are policewomen. Detectives. They will help take your daughter to the hospital. They will spare you the paperwork."

The father watched Jack silently.

"Sometimes women understand women better," Jack added. The father took a breath and silently gave in, stepping back as the female detectives followed the grandmother to the far bedroom.

"Go with them," he said to the girl's mother.

Jack stood with the uncle and the father, the three men quiet in the kitchen area. Jack could see the detectives working the girl in the bedroom, reassuring her. He saw the panda's legs swinging, shifting in the girl's embrace.

In five minutes they'll have her enroute to Downtown Hospital or Gouveneur General. Administer a rape kit. Capture DNA. One of the SCU would process the crime scene, double-check with a flashlight, and again in daylight.

The girl hugged the panda as she left with the tall detective, throwing Jack a sorrowful look, on her small face a sad and fearful smile. The mother went along.

Alone with the uncle at the door, Jack said, "I'll need a photograph of your niece." The uncle gave him one from his wallet, a school picture with a sky-blue background.

"Her father is talking about going to the elders of his village association," the uncle said, "to get something going."

Jack knew what he meant, that they'd do their own investigation. He gave the uncle a Detective's Endowment Association card. "Call me if you hear anything," Jack said, before he entered the elevator.

* * *

The orange glow of the sunset was barely above the horizon of the West Side as he walked back toward the stationhouse and the Fury. He felt a growl in his stomach, and for a second considered taking his meal break, but he had no appetite. Instead, the knot that was clenching in his gut reminded him how vicious the world was to the innocents who could not defend themselves. *How does a cop get help from a community that has no faith in officers of the law?"*

He went past the groups of black gangsta toughs gathering in the projects, all do-rags and gold-capped teeth, and turned his thoughts to the colors of the neon lights blinking in Chinatown in the distance. In his heart, filled with hate, he was wishing he could put his hands on this cowardly unknown molester of children and slowly choke the life from him.

Lucky

Tat "Lucky" Louie sat on the edge of the futon in the dark bedroom of the Bridgeview condo and gathered his clothes around him. He strapped on a gold Rolex and dressed in a hurry.

Lucky was a *dailo*—elder brother and leader—of the brotherhood of the Ghost Legion. In another mob he would have been a *capo*, maybe a lieutenant. The On Yee bigshots, rivals of the Hip Ching, gave him a piece of their two-card parlors, and he had two young crews that answered to him. One crew for the streets, a couple dozen wiry teenage toughs, all Hong Kong Chinese, gun-crazy and wild-eyed. The second crew was for special jobs: kidnapping, enforcing, robbery, whatever became necessary. A dozen real warriors, refugees from hellholes across Southeast

Asia: a half-breed Thai boy, two Cambodians, six Vietnamese Chinese, and Kongo, the big dark Malay who never spoke, who always had the cut-off scatter gun on his hip. When the Ghosts went out on a war party, it was this crew of hotheads their enemies feared most, *his* pack of crazed sociopaths.

The morning light crept in along the edges of the window blinds, and he stepped into his black Versace loafers. He left the gunmetal-gray silk jacket open, loose-fitting cover for a five-ten frame that was twenty pounds overweight. It had gone to flab, new gut hanging where muscle had given way to beer and fatty fast-food dinners. It didn't matter, he didn't need to fight anymore. He had *face* on the streets, and face was everything.

He slipped a box-cutter into his jacket pocket.

The Fukienese, he thought, didn't care about face, and needed to be taught a lesson. Their Fuk Ching lowboys wanted a gang-bang over East Broadway, they were going to get it. He knew how, but that would come later, after he'd fixed it with Uncle Four, to keep the Black Dragons out of the way.

There was a truce on.

He *was* lucky. He had outlived those above him who had burned brighter, lived faster, died younger. When the Feds had cleaned out the last of the Ghost Legion's upper ranks ten years earlier, he'd inherited his position by default. The Legion had to rebuild, and he'd been all they had left.

The door slammed behind him, and he went down, watching the elevator light drop the five levels. The new day was a pale flat wash of morning, broken by clouds, a filtering of sunlight. He turned out to Mott Street and quickened his pace, wanting to get to *fay por*—fat lady—Fat Lily's mahjong parlor early, while the girls were still fresh and clean. He didn't like the idea of walking into sloppy fifths, behind some phlegmy Hakkanese butcher. It didn't matter how many men the girls had had the night before. Each day was new.

Although the Ghosts operated under the banner of the On Yee, the biggest, wealthiest, and most prestigious Chinatown tong, Lucky realized he had to navigate with great care the treacherous alliances with old-timers like Uncle Four, who controlled the Hip Chings. He knew the Legion had to be wary of new and formidable foes from Mainland China, Southeast Asia, and Taiwan.

He knew that when the politics shifted in Hong Kong's secret societies, the triads, the shit usually slammed into the fan on Mott Street.

The On Yee was a businessmen's Benevolent Association, the Number One high roller in America, a coast-to-coast secret society no workingman was able to join. They sneered at the ship-jumpers, the waiters and dishwashers, the laundrymen, who joined the rival Hip Chings. In Chinatown, no business could open without paying *deem heunq yau*, bribes, to the On Yee membership.

Lucky knew their leadership was younger and more liberal, willing to take chances by working with Italians, and other *lo fan*. He had seen elder leaders come and go, and less senior members disappear outright. On Yee membership was what he wanted, but only on *his* terms.

He saw the spiraling barber stripe down the street. He was almost there.

Over the years, he had developed a lumbering gait like a bear, trying to accommodate his bulk, resulting in an awkward strutting bop. He thought it was like a cool pimp roll, throwing his weight around.

He thought it intimidated his enemies.

The dirty brick building at 94 Elizabeth was a whorehouse disguised as a barbershop at street level, a mahjong club on the second floor, a massage joint on the third.

The barbershop had a backroom behind a red curtain, for that extra trim, or blow job. They played high-stakes mahjong on two, where Fat Lily Wong usually kept watch over the premises. She was the eldest daughter of a Hip Ching officer.

The third floor had a sauna, two sofa beds, a set of massage gurneys on wheels, and four cubicles with covered mattresses. There was a condom machine on the wall.

Lucky went past the spinning candycane barber pole, pressed the bell, waited while Fat Lily checked him out via the surveillance camera. After a moment he was buzzed in.

Normally there were five girls working upstairs, Malaysians and Vietnamese. On Friday nights and weekends they added a crew of Korean girls, so they totaled a dozen in all, upstairs and downstairs. These girls serviced over three hundred men a week.

Lucky liked to rotate girls; sometimes he came here twice a week. He didn't care about the hundred a bang for the nasty sex, figured it was all part of the same dirty money circling around his life. It was like a perk, he thought, for the tension he had to deal with.

She told Lucky her name was Leena. She was a dusty-colored Malay girl with large brown nipples that cried out to be sucked. Lucky ran his tongue over the areolas in a circular motion, making tiny bites on the nipples as he went, sucking, bringing her body jerking up off the bed, her hands holding his head to her breasts, moaning now. Her body quivered on the cool sheets, her arms pulling him down into her, clutching at his lower back, floating over his buttocks, all the while moaning as he thrust in and out of her hot wetness.

He raised her legs into the air, held them by the ankles, spread them open into a V and rode his hardness into her, the wet slap of his groin against her bottom bringing sharp, loud groans, then pleading whispers.

When it got hotter, he turned her over, entered her from above. She wailed as Lucky pounded against her buttocks, begging now. *He loved loving her.* He slipped his member out, brushed its slick hard head around her velvet lips, slipped it back inside. She gasped and he thrust hard and long, then softly, gently. He put his tongue inside her, licked around her hard little button, plunged himself back in. She just kept coming, convulsive spasms fighting for breath, coming even as he exploded, then shivering soft whispers, pleading, full of want and fulfillment.

Later he cradled her like a baby, nibbled on her ear. She turned over and took his spent member in her hand, caressing it, nestling her head into his throat, licking it.

They were two players, playing each other.

"I love you," he whispered, checking his Rolex.

"Sure," she agreed, "sure you do," giving him face.

"I'll see you tomorrow," he whispered, his tongue in her ear.

"Sure," she said, "I'll be waiting."

His hands went over her breast one last time.

She flicked up a cigarette and watched him making ready to go. When he finished dressing, he placed the crisp Ben Franklin on the bed next to her, kissed her on the head, and left the musty cool of the little room.

Sanctuary

Confucius Towers was a forty-five-story crescent-shaped brick complex.

Uncle Four took the express elevator to apartment H, twenty stories above the heart of Chinatown. He heard the clatter of ivory tiles as he approached his door. No surprise there.

His wife, *Tam tai*, former Taiwanese starlet now longtime mahjong wife was holding court at the squared *wong fa lee* antique table, surrounded by a much younger gaggle of *siew lai lai,* ladies of leisure, chatting her up over cocktails and seafood—*siew ma*—dumplings that were displayed on matching pearl-studded mahogany folding trays.

The wispy romance of Hong Kong pop music floated off a compact disk and spread throughout the spacious living room, around the carved Ming armoire, past the set of zitan-wood Imperial chairs, a ballad just loud enough so they never heard Uncle Four enter, closing the door with a pickpocket's touch. He stood behind the lacquered rosewood and inlaid-jade screen that set off the foyer and pictured them.

Wife, almost fifty, her hair dyed blacker than *fot choy*, moss threads, and teased perfect above curved eyebrows redrawn daily. Pancake on the crow's feet at the corners of eyes blinking out from heavy shadow and liner, leaving the red gash of her mouth at a restless angle. She wore gold on one wrist, jade on the other; an aging actress in her sunset performance on the Chinatown stage.

Too much perfume, he could smell it from the door, streaming from the four women at the table. They were talking at each other in choppy, patterned phrases.

Loo *je*, sister Loo, was married to the treasurer of the Hip Ching, giving her the unofficial rank of *daai ga je*, elder sister, in their entourage. She wore clothes from The Limited, and spoke in a mannish style.

"Business has been good," she said. "Should be bigger bonuses this year."

Mak *mui*, her cousin, who was engaged to a senior Black Dragon, cooed, "Wonderful, another gold bracelet for me."

Shirley, which they pronounced, *surly,* was the oldest. "Sisters," she said, "life is good. Jade and diamonds for everyone. A toast!"

The women clinked glasses and drank, settled back into their game, slapping the mahjong tiles back and forth across the table.

Silly women, thought Uncle Four behind the screen. When he married the second time, it had appeared to be a fortunate match. Using Tam *tai's* connections in the Taiwanese film industry, he'd established a chain of Chinese videotape rental outlets that stretched from the Chinatowns in San Francisco to New York, from Toronto to Florida.

They had no children.

He had a teenaged daughter from his first marriage and had wanted nothing more to do with children after that. This had suited Tam *tai* fine. At the time they married she was already in her late-thirties, and he knew, secretly, that she was barren. He gave her a share of the video business and the skim money from the Ting Lee Beauty Salon, in which he was also a partner. She made the collections personally, every week on Monday.

Now, a decade after exchanging vows and toasts, they lived separate lives in the same apartment. Separate bedrooms, separate schedules, and separate vices. The only values left to share were money and jewelry, and never enough of either.

Pung! Mak *mui* shouted, grabbing the discarded tile. She splayed out her row of thin blocks and grinned.

"*Mun wu,*" she laughed. A full house.

The others groaned and collapsed their hands, then threw dollar bills at her.

The little ivory blocks were crashed and shoved together into a large pile.

Uncle Four stepped out from behind the screen amid the racket and entered the living room. There was a short silence as the surprised women turned their eyes to him. His wife raised her chin, smiled, said nothing.

He murmured *lo por*, wife, at her and nodded at the others, turned and headed for his bedroom at the far end. *Lo por* drained her vodka tonic as he passed, the others watching him. When he turned to close the door, their attention shifted quickly back to the table, his wife already stacking the tiles, quietly forming a wall.

She glanced at the closing door and listened for the click of the lock that closed off the world of her estranged *lo gung*.

Billy Tofu

The sky had drifted back to a leaden gray when Jack rolled onto Mott, parking the Dodge Fury up the street from On Yee headquarters, around the block from the stationhouse. He saw the busloads of weekend tourists deboarding into the streets, mixing with locals waking to morning errands, and the taking of tea, *yum cha*.

The tourists moved along in a huddling line, bought T-shirts and fake Chanel scarves, and were herded along the three blocks back to their buses idling at the edge of Chatham Square.

Jack sat in the car. His visit to Pa's apartment, the photographs, all had him thinking of those three rudderless years of his life in the Tofu King. And of Billy Bow.

Billy was the last friend Jack still had in Chinatown from the old crowd. Everyone else had married, moved to the suburbs, came

49

to town only on special occasions to visit their parents, grandparents, whoever was abandoned in Chinatown.

Billy was still there, and whenever Jack was in the neighborhood, he went by the Tofu King for a fresh *dao jeong*, soy bean milk, and to shoot the breeze with him.

They'd become fast friends in those years together in the back of the shop, cooking, slopping beans. The shop was smaller then, and it wasn't until Billy's grandfather renovated the upstairs and expanded into the backyard that it became the Tofu King. That was ten years ago, when Jack left. Billy was still there, thirteen years a captive in his father's business.

And since then Billy'd become hard and cynical. He was divorced, paying child support, and when he was two boilermakers deep, he'd call himself "a deadbeat Chinaman with two princess daughters and a dead-end job."

He'd wanted to be a writer, an actor, something creative, but nothing went his way. He tried college but couldn't keep up. He took the tests for civil service but they weren't hiring Chinamen with nothing on their resume except ten years in a bean-curd shop.

So there he was, drowning in bean milk, and no way out.

This time, Jack had called Billy to confirm permission to post composite sketches from the SCU, which had arrived together with a note that said the girl's pregnancy test had come back negative. He'd need to post one sketch inside and one outside of the Tofu King. Some stores considered it bad luck to bring a sign of such an event, an evil presence, into their places of business.

Billy was okay with it.

Outside the Tofu King, a man wearing a white apron sold fried Chinese turnip cakes, attracting a crowd beneath the white plastic fluorescent sign that said tofu, *puto*. Wholesale and Retail.

Business was brisk. Inside the shop the walls were white tile all the way around. The near wall opened to a window on the street where they sold cold bean milk and hot tofu custard to passersby. Four fifty-gallon barrels of soft tofu lined the left wall, four more barrels of hard tofu on the right. *Foo jook*, bean curd strips, took shape in the large water tank in back, past the refrigerated counter with the *bok tong go*, sweet rice cakes, and the *gee cheung fun*, noodles.

Six workers were on the floor, three of them plastic-wrapping the white bricks of tofu for local groceries. For the restaurants, the workers packed the ivory bricks in water, fitting them snugly into ten-gallon tin cans.

It all started with the beans.

They arrived once a month, sixteen tons of soybeans via Jacky Chew, the trucker. The beans came out of Indiana in tractor-trailer loads, in hundred-pound sacks, twenty-thousand beans each sack. They soaked the beans upstairs, then they were ground down and cooked, mixed, and at different levels in the process became firm tofu, silken tofu, tofu sticks, tofu skins, and soy bean milk drink. The smell was thick upstairs, hanging in the hot air, suffocating. This went on twenty-four hours a day.

Jack looked down the street and saw the line of empty carts moving into the Tofu King. He took a roll of composite sketches of the rapist from the glove compartment and checked his watch. It was ten-thirty.

The sky darkened and a few Ghosts appeared on the street. Jack watched them, four youths with streaked hair and leather jackets, as they took up positions on the corner. Behind them, farther down the street, Jack saw a soft doughy-faced Lucky, his one-time friend Tat Louie, behind sunglasses, chatting easily with Uncle Four, making accommodating gestures with his hands.

Jack narrowed his eyes at them, the Pell Street big shot, Ghost Legion gang leader. An arrogant power meeting on the streets they ruled.

A few more Ghosts came onto the street, took up space on the opposite corner. They observed all that passed, signaling to one another across the street with cat whistles, woofing at pretty girls, flexing the tattoos on their skinny arms.

The two leaders shook hands, and then the Big Uncle ambled down Bayard Street.

Jack watched the Ghosts strut off, keeping his eyes on Lucky, who turned and stared through his black glasses momentarily at the Fury. Lucky raised his middle finger and waved it loosely, sneered, then crossed the street and disappeared around the corner.

A tinge of sadness colored Jack's vision, but he pushed away the feeling it brought. Tat Louie was a stranger now, deep on the other side of the law.

Jack grabbed the roll of composite sketches and slid out of the car.

Inside the Tofu King, he saw Billy stamping about, waving a yellow paper in his hand, cursing, "niggers with badges, them motherfuckers." He slammed the paper down on the counter, turned, and saw Jack. He shook his head and frowned, the corners of his mouth turning down.

Jack stood ready to listen, his face sympathetic, nodding.

"The Department of Health, *Wealth,* I should say, came yesterday," Billy hissed. "Then this motherfucker gives me a ticket 'cause there's some papers in the street. Told 'im it wasn't my shit, must've blown down from the corner, from a car or something, you know? The kid swept this morning already. What the fuck you want me to do? Put him out there all day with a broom in his hand? Motherfucker says 'Eighteen inches from the curb, *bro*. You got garbage, you got a violation.' Just like that, the motherfucker. I called him a spear-chucking, watermelon-eating black cocksucker. He laughs and walks away. Shit. Gonna cost me seventy-five. That's a lotta *dao jeung*. Damn it, City Hall makes a killing off of Chinamen. Chinatown is a goddamn gold mine to them. The traffic pricks cut tickets by intimidation. They know most Chinese don't speak enough English to argue. Health and Sanitation target the restaurants. Department of Buildings, Fire Code inspectors, they go after the construction crews. Plainclothes issues summonses to sidewalk peddlers, grocers, the gift shops. Everyone down here's paying some fine, pay-offs not included. It's bullshit. No other minority group in the city pays off like the Chinese do. How come we don't have no NAACP?"

Billy paused to catch his breath. "Man, the city's got more niggers on the payroll than Welfare, and they all drop down here like the black plague, *getting paid,* busting on the yellow man."

Jack shook his head, then Billy grinned. "I'm telling you, Jack, I gotta get out of this business." He tossed Jack a bean milk.

"Write it off, Billy," Jack said. "It comes with the turf." He gave Billy a few of the composite sketches. "I need you to post these. Show 'em to your workers. See if they hear anything."

"This the guy, huh? The Chinatown Rapist?"

"That's our impression of the guy."

"What a scumbag. I'll post 'em Jack, sure, but I don't know."

"What?"

"There's a thousand guys out there look like this."

"We gotta start somewhere." Jack looked out the window, scanned the street where Lucky had been.

"Sure, I'll keep my ears open," Billy said. "What else is up?"

Jack put down the milk. "You seen Tat around, Billy?"

"Tat?" Billy's brow knitted. "That low life? Yeah, I seen him. Runs around with them punks following him."

"They ever come in here?"

"Tried to *sell* me one of the fucking hundred-dollar orange trees on Chinese New Year."

"What happened?"

"Dad was paid up with the On Yee and they called them off."

"Good."

"Otherwise I'd of blown them away. Tat don't fucken scare me."

Jack watched him, said, "Where's he hang now?"

Billy grimaced. "What you want that scumball for?"

"Nothing personal, Billy."

"Cops and hoods, huh?" Billy smirked. "The good turn bad, the bad gets worse. You sure like stepping in shit, Jack."

"I know it," Jack agreed. "Supposed to be good luck." He offered a dollar for the drink.

"Don't embarrass me, Jacky," Billy said sternly, and Jack put his cash away.

"Try the basements on Mott, Number Nine, Number Sixty-Six," Billy said quietly.

"Okay, one more thing."

"Shoot."

"You got any cardboard boxes? I'm cleaning out the old place."

Billy read Jack's eyes. "Oh, yeah, I heard. Sorry about your old man." He paused. "He was a right guy. A standup Chinaman, Jack."

"Yeah," Jack said very quietly. "That he was."

"Come by later, I'll tell the kid, put some aside."

"Thanks."

"You okay with it?"

"Yeah, I'm okay."

They were silent a moment, then Billy's ire came back and he yelled at some of the new workers as a tractor-trailer rolled in out front.

"Damn *jookies*," he said, referring to the cadre of newly arrived teenage Fukienese he had working upstairs in the hot room. "They just don't get it. I told them, 'Learn English. You won't have to run away every time the *gwai-lo* comes in. You can do better. You don't have to be stuck working here.'"

He took a deep breath. "You think they listen? 'How come *you* still here?' the wiseguy says."

A crew of the young wetbacks sauntered toward the street and the tractor trailer. Billy shook his head at them, said derisively, through his frown, "Look at 'em, clothes don't match but they perm their hair. At lunchtime they squat in the alleyway and pick their noses and spit clams on the wall. They talk too loud, and they laugh like hyenas. *Refugees.*"

"Good help is hard to find," Jack sympathized.

"*Cheap* good help is hard to find," Billy countered. "If it weren't for me, they'd still be in the village, wearing them rubber sandals, *gong hen*, the shit still between their toes." He watched them unloading the trailer, said, "You're in America, I keep telling 'em. Be American."

"Yeah," Jack twisted, "Be like us. Misery loves company." They slapped palms and Jack added, "One last thing, I need to know about the Fuk Ching."

Just then it got busy in the shop, a sudden line of Midwestern tourists gawking at the Yellows, each buying souvenir packs of sweet tofu cake.

Jack wised to Billy's busy situation.

Billy patted him on the shoulder, tipped his chin at him and said, "Later, Grandpa's, around midnight." Then he moved off into the hubbub, toward the truck.

Jack finished the *dao jeung* and went out the side door, past the helpers unloading the sacks of beans, past the deliverymen with their carts full of *cheung fun,* broad noodles. He took a last look at Billy, who was barking orders into the air, then he put on his shades, and slipped into the Chinatown afternoon.

Old Woman

Because of the nature of the crime, as well as the race of the victim and the perpetrator, Jack took it personally, felt the case needed special attention. So he carried the victim photographs and the perp sketches down the side streets, on his day off, on neighborhood time.

He came off of Mott onto Bayard, walking briskly toward the Tombs detention facility, toward the gaggle of old women gathered on the corner of Columbus Park.

The fortune-telling ladies, elderly women who would have appeared more at home in a Toishan dirt village, congregated by the entrance to the park, squatting on low wooden footstools, spreading out their charts, drawings, herbs, the tools of their divinations. Some had little umbrellas raised against the mist.

Jack sought out Ah Por, a wizened old woman wrapped in a quilted *meen naap* silk jacket, her tiny feet in sweat socks and kung fu slippers. She squatted among the old women, on her footstool, quietly chatting with another ancient spirit.

The old women looked at Jack with great curiosity, though they were careful to avoid the rudeness of staring. They watched him sidewise, framing him in their peripheral vision. When he stepped up to Ah Por, there by the fence, the old women moved aside to allow him in, then re-formed around him, all wondering what this young Chinese man wanted from their eldest sister.

Jack had remembered Pa going to Ah Por many years after Ma died. His visits were to get lucky words and numbers to play the Chinese Lottery, or to hear of good fortune. Now he was coming to Ah Por with victim photographs of young girls, Chinese girls with long black hair.

There was neither recognition nor fear in Ah Por's eyes. She simply accepted him with a sweeping graceful look, and he squatted down on one knee and held the two pictures in front of her.

"Tell me about them," he said.

She took the photographs and studied them intently, then turned them upside down, narrowed her eyes again.

Two preteen girls who looked enough alike that they might be sisters. Preppie school jackets, big smiles grinning out at the world, deep obsidian eyes.

"This one is shy," said Ah Por. "She holds back her laughter. The other is bright, a brave girl."

Ah Por took up her cup, rolled a bundle of bamboo sticks in her alm, letting them fall back into the cup, rolling them again, dropping them again. She did this for thirty seconds, did it with the practiced grace of someone telling rosary beads.

She bobbed her head in a slow rhythmic nod, closed her eyes. *Tai Seung*, thought Jack, the art of reading faces.

Ah Por awoke with a shudder. When she rattled the sticks in her cup, they all seemed to rise and dance near the rim. One stick shot out and it was numbered seventeen. She consulted her red booklet with the black ink-brushed Chinese characters, the *Book of Fortunes*.

She stroked the pages with her long thumbnail, ran it down the columns of proverbs, tapped it on a section of fortunes.

"The first one," she said softly, "will marry a rich man and have two boys." Jack leaned in with his ear.

"The second will do well in school, make a lot of money."

Jack said nothing when she glanced at him.

"But there is something bad following them, isn't there?"

Jack said quietly, "A bad man has hurt them."

Ah Por caught her breath. "Oh dear."

She repeated it several times and then there was a long pause, her eyes looking distant when she said, "I see fire, and someone with small ears."

"The bad man?" Jack asked.

"Fire," she repeated, voice so faint it was almost gone, "and small ears."

Jack got up, gave her five dollars. He thanked her and made his way through the circle of old women.

Nothing, he thought. He had nothing but riddles and proverbs, spirit mumbo jumbo and witchcraft.

And someone was out there raping young Chinese girls.

Nothing, he groused, as he came back around the park, passing through the queues of junket buses, caravans loaded down for Atlantic City, fat with Chinatown cash.

On Canal Street, the last of the gray day was fading out around the *gung chong por,* factory women, slogging their plastic bags of groceries toward the subway.

Jack turned onto Mott and headed back toward the Fury. He still had Billy's boxes to get, and frustration once again fueled the need to get away from Chinatown.

Change

He took the Brooklyn Bridge across the East River, felt the rumble leave the tires as they bit into the steel grating, the car making a blurring dull buzz-saw sound as it descended toward land.

He drove down the sloping streets south to the Forties, to Sunset Park, the newest Chinatown and his new neighborhood. He had moved out here a year ago, only the second place he could call his own, the first being the Chinatown railroad flat he had shared with Wing Lee that teenage summer before his friend was murdered.

Once a Scandinavian community called Finntown, Sunset Park had become largely Latino, but in the 1990s, the Chinese garment industry had followed low rents out of Manhattan, settled into old warehouses and factories here, blazing the way for the thirty thousand Malaysians and Fukienese who came afterward. Their food shops ran along the main streets, bringing to South Brooklyn the aroma of the Asian hot pot.

Jack took a studio apartment in a renovated red-brick condominium building. It had a view of the harbor and the Bush Terminal docks and, ten minutes across the river, it felt like another world, light-years from the Chinatown he'd grown up in.

He liked the sight of the ships, the freighters that glided across the water, nestled into their docks by the tugs bumping alongside. The way the sunsets played over the harbor was like new medicine, soothing, long overdue.

Now, however, there was nothing but darkness spreading across the overcast horizon.

He poured a Johnny Black into a tumbler and chased it with

beer, felt an easy peacefulness settling over him as he scanned the studio.

Even now, a year after he'd moved in, he still kept things to a minimum, mostly portable, transient, *disposable* items, his life in flux. The spirit of his father, the sojourner, was still in his blood. He leaned back in the recliner, taking a visual inventory of the room.

There was the convertible sofa bed, a Trinitron TV on a plastic Parsons table, and a halogen floor lamp. At the end of the table was a compact digital clock/radio/stereo CD/tape player, and on the windowsill sat a miniature orange tree.

Across from the kitchenette stood a black folding table bearing stacks of *Newsweek, Guns & Ammo,* and a disconnected beeper he'd bought so Pa could call him, but he never had. There were a few books: *Wing Chun,* the deadly art of thrusting fingers, and *Choy Li Fut Kung Fu.* Beneath all that was a bar stool; a pair of dusty Rollerblades rested against the baseboard.

He had a Mr. Coffee, a wok, a twenty-five-pound sack of rice in a Tupperware barrel.

The only thing on the walls was a poster he'd gotten from the Metropolitan Museum of Art, the Japanese one with the wave crashing.

In the bank, he had the eight thousand dollars he'd saved. He had no outstanding payments or mortgage debt, his financial life was balanced on a cop's salary. His was a workingman's life, so much like Pa's, a slave to his paycheck, never knowing the luxurious lifestyle of the people he was duty bound to serve and protect.

His thoughts flashed wide and scattered, his mind adrift, anchorless. He ate takeout from Eighth Avenue, reloaded the black knapsack, felt he needed to finish something so he finished the Johnny Walker and fell out, puzzling over the old family photographs with the radio on.

The Easy Score

The Yee Bot was a Fuk Ching gambling-spot setup in a tenement storefront, one of many in a long row of walk-up tenements fading to the far end of the street. Lucky knew this end of East Broadway, knew it was the Chinese frontier, where they had pushed into areas traditionally Jewish, now mixed with spics and niggers and squashed up against the East River into the Projects.

He knew the tenements connected along their backyards, like a spine running between them, some of the passageways blocked up or gated. He had broken into some of these apartments when he was younger, terrorized the neighborhood until one day he entered a place he thought was Chinese but was actually Puerto Rican and almost got shot dead. He stayed clear of that end of East Broadway until he hooked up with the Ghosts, quietly watching the neighborhood fill with Fukienese businesses.

The Yee Bot or "Twenty-eight" spot was a local hangout of the Fuk Ching gang, located on what was technically a Fuk Ching street—that is the Fuk Benevolent Association was located nearby, its entrance fronted by matching larger-than-life Foo dogs.

The Fuk Chings claimed to have thousands of members everywhere, bristling with heavy-duty weaponry and itching to do battle. On this particular end of East Broadway, however, they had only thirty-nine members, mostly *lan jai*, busted boys who were the remnants of splinter gangs affiliated with the Benevolent

Association's darker elements—gambling, drugs, nightclubs and prostitution. Rumor was the gang had split violently over profits.

Lucky remembered the "Twenty-eight" had big gates up front, knew lots of heavy-duty protection was there. The Fuk Chings had started frisking patrons with electronic wands, believed they could stop weapons from getting in and challenging them. So far they had been right.

But Lucky knew the tiny backyards between the tenements, where the rain gutters emptied out, were used for storage of cleaning materials. He knew the backyard, the backdoor, was the way in.

Ghost spies had brought back a diagram.

The "house," nerve center of the gambling operation, was located in a recessed room halfway down a long hall. It was protected on both sides. All of the house action, cash and dealers, came out of that big room, which could be isolated by electric rollup gates that slid up into the ceiling. Everything in the joint was stacked toward the front. Lucky saw it all with wicked clarity: the backdoor was the way in.

Lucky crossed the rooftop, scaled a short wall and dropped onto the adjacent rooftop landing below. He was confronted by a brick wall, reached in back of it and found a niche behind it. He felt around, started taking loose bricks out. Another niche. More bricks came out. Then he touched it, a bundle wrapped in plastic. He unwrapped it, revealing his favorite weapon, the Cyborg Bullpup, a nasty nine-shot twelve-gauge shotgun made up like the hi-tech tactical-assault something the SWAT guys used. It had a black-rubber stock and a top handle, black all over with front and back grips, ventilated shroud, the works.

Lucky racked it, triggered and re-racked it, in love with the sound of metal sliding and catching. Shotguns couldn't be traced, and besides, he had filed off all the serial numbers, smooth as porcelain. The Cyborg weighed ten pounds, heavy to carry, but he had it on an elastic shoulder sling that kept the monster tight to his side, under the white smock he wore, his right hand, his gun hand, inside on the trigger.

The Mossberg 590 Cyborg Bullpup. Cost him two hundred, a steal. Bought it off some Haitian junkie who said it was used in a drug war in Washington Heights, wanted to dump it, probably had bodies on it. Lucky bought it anyway, knowing he'd never leave a trace on it. Use it, discard it. One time only and that time had come. The rest of his mad-dog crazies had cheap nine-millimeter pistols they could pop and drop. Throwaways.

For ammunition, Lucky liked the Remington SPs; multi-range shot shells, it said on the box. Ten plastic shotgun shells filled with buffered, copper-plated shot. *Keep out of reach of children,* Lucky read with a grin. He liked the SPs because each shot shell contained different size shot, some smaller pellets to scatter the field, flush 'em out, then larger pellets to bring them down *while delivering optimum energy and penetration at longer ranges,* the box said. Yeah, thought Lucky, settle them motherfuckers quick. People didn't like to argue with a shotgun.

Lucky's war party carried no identification. Should they ever be caught or killed, they didn't want anything leading back to the Ghost Legion. This way, they'd divvy up the loot among themselves, instead of with the entire gang, twelve ways being a lot bigger than seventy-seven, plus a percentage to the big shots. Also, since most of the crazies were illegals, they didn't need to be ID'd and deported. They carried extra ammunition and backed up their throwaway Star pistols with hot Hi-Tecs.

A quarter-to-twelve, strike when the cops were caught between shifts. If things went good, they'd be out before midnight. The entire crew was ready now, Lucky leading them under a moonless night toward the far end of East Broadway.

It was Saturday night and the joint was rocking. The old man guard who sat in the dimly lit back space by the metal folding table, with its electric pots of coffee and tea, took in all the activity in the Yee Bot. He sat almost motionless, watching the gambling from the distance, blinking only when the smoke from the cigarette dangling from the corner of his lips curled up into his eyes. Behind him was a small doorway. Occasionally, he'd glance back to check out the sounds of kitchen clatter coming from the restaurant across the alley.

Lucky came over the top of the backyard wall, a rolling black blur over the razor wire. He sneaked across the tops of the crates piled up there. Now, with all the crazies poised behind him, he racked the BullPup.

The old man cocked his ear to the backdoor, listened for a long second. He turned his head around and scanned the back area framing the door, dropping his right hand into his waistband, to the .38 Blackhawk under his vest. He listened and looked for another long moment. More clatter came from the restaurant kitchen. He took a deep drag on his cigarette, hissed the smoke out in a long stream, satisfied now, and turned back to the action on the floor.

The next thing he saw was a man dressed in a white smock, the kind that butchers or kitchen help wore, with a white cap down over his eyes. He had in his hands a package in brown butcher paper that indicated he was delivering goods. The old man was frozen, silent. *How did he get in here?* he thought. Then everything went dark inside his head as Lucky blackjacked him behind the right ear with his free hand, and watched him sag forward. The crazies rushed inside past them, backed up by Kongo, the silent one.

Lucky pressed into the side of his coat, releasing the BullPup's safety. He took two steps inside the "Twenty-eight," brought it up toward the ceiling, and squeezed the trigger.

The first blast blew out lights in the sheetrock ceiling, froze everyone in an eyeblink, as the Ghosts laid the drop on the Fuk Chings at the tables, taking their Makarovs and revolvers. Lucky racked the BullPup again, herded everyone toward the front as the crazies scooped money off the tables, overturning them so they blocked the rolldown gates from dropping in front of the house.

Lucky yanked the terrified manager off the floor and shoved him into the house room, where the dealers were cowering. He slipped the BullPup into its sling at his side and drew a pistol from his shoulder holster. He kicked the manager down next to the safe and smacked him with barrel of the Colt. The man whimpered and Lucky smacked him again, harder. Lucky cocked the Colt and pressed it into the man's ear, eyeballing the fallen dealers.

"Open up or die here," Lucky snarled into the terrorized silence.

Two crazies stepped forward and pistol-whipped the dealers, their blood splattering the money scattered on the floor. The manager saw death in their pinpoint eyes and spun the safe dial with shaking fingers, left, right, then yanked the door open.

Lucky's wristwatch started beeping, the four-minute warning, as the Ghosts shoved stacks of money into a duffel bag. They tossed smoke bombs as they left. Lucky slid out the BullPup and waited as the crazies made their way over the razor wire. He squeezed off a load as he stepped out back, no arguments chasing him. In a second he was over the top, following the sound of footsteps quickly retreating into the dark distance, with bloody Fuk Ching money in his pockets.

Midnight.

Driver

Johnny slept through the morning behind drawn shades, showered, rubbed mousse in his coal-black trim, and combed it straight back. He put on a turtleneck and a leather vest, drove down Eighth Avenue and out of Brooklyn. Then he ate lunch from a takeout box while waiting for the Lincoln to clear the track at the Broadway Car Wash.

The buffing gang put a glow on the black-and-chrome body, vacuumed the interior, cleared the air of cigar smells, and exchanged the odor of stale perfume for that of pine and new leather.

He booked two afternoon trips, one to Belmont, the other out to LaGuardia. Mona's pick-up wasn't until nine-thirty, so he had time to kill.

He purred the Continental toward Grand Street, skirting gridlock traffic until he could see the queues of people waiting for the *van jai*—passenger vans—back to Queens. Pick off a few going to Flushing, he figured, and he'd set himself up for the races at Belmont.

Cheen Money

The Harmonious Garden was a cramped fast-food sit-down on Baxter Way that had a backdoor leading out to a cinder-block bunker slapped up in the courtyard between buildings. The bunker had a back exit, leading through the building in its rear to the boulevard beyond.

One of its walls featured video poker and slot machines. Opposite them, the Ghost boys sat on bar stools with their portable phones and ran a sports book next to the two thirty-inch color TV monitors flashing the Knicks, the Giants, the Rangers.

They ran three card tables featuring Chinese Poker. The On Yee covered the joint with pocket money. Twenty-four hours. They kept on hand six cases of Johnny Walker Black, eight eighths of Ecuadorian flake, and quarter-ounce plastics of sensemilla smoke for the day's customers.

Lucky went through the restaurant into the crowded bunker, where he found a seat at the card tables. Above the noise from the TV sets and the electronic ping of the video games, he picked up on the rough chatter of the gamblers:

"The cok-sooka won six thousand last week. Took four straight turns at House. Kept eating heads and tails."

"Took *everybody's* money."

"Big game later, the laundry boys from Boston, and that Jap high roller from Atlantic City."

"The Thailand Brothers are coming."

"They're closing two tables for the Lucky Eight."

"A hundred a section."

Some players, busted, fell out of the deal with *dew ka ma ga hei motherfucker* curses, and Lucky edged up along the table. He wanted to spread some of the loot from the Yee Bot rip-off into his own joints, spur up the action. He laid his stack of U.S. Grants behind the House box, scanned the bets in the four squares, and waited for the cards to turn up. The dealer took the thirteen cards and opened them in his palm, the other bettors working their hands. Lucky set up the three sections, rearranging the suits, the pairs. The best he had was a pair of jacks, a pair of kings, and a straight flush.

The straight flush would likely win the last section, and he decided to play the jacks up front, figuring the two pairs too weak in the middle.

Lucky watched as his cards took heads and tails, raiding cash from the Thais and Malaysians betting the four boxes.

Lucky let the winnings roll.

The dealer ran through a three-hour rotation of players and before the dinner shift had taken three thousand eighty out of the squares.

When the sun set, Lucky went down to the Bowery outskirts, the desolate streets leading out beyond Chinatown where it rubbed raw against the rest of Loisaida and the Alphabets. He entered the storefront with its window gate down, next to the bodega. One of Flavio's places. Spread the dirty money among the clients. Goodwill for Flavio, a kilo-a-week buyer of Ghost Number Four heroin.

Inside, Lucky gave the *mommy* fifty dollars, looking over the partition to scan the *Latina crikas*—whores—seated on folding chairs under the sickly green-blue light of lava lamps. Some of the whores had thighs heavy with cellulite inside fishnet stockings, bean-bloated bellies under spandex, hard faces pushing the far side of forty.

The *mommy* gave him a playing card, a yellow jack. Men were waiting about, sexual tension leaned up against the walls, and then a few more girls came out of the back maze of cubicles, carrying baskets of mouthwash, condoms, KY Jelly, and paper towels. There were Cubans, a Venezuelan, a Panamanian, a Colombian, but mostly they were Dominicans fresh off the tarmac at LaGuardia, jetting in via the Santo Domingo pipeline.

For the merciless dollar they'd surrender themselves up to

desperate men they'd rendered faceless, shapeless, colorless, just a trick tube of flesh invading their vaginas, their mouths, but not their souls.

The Panamanian. Young and tall, bottle-blond. He gave her the playing card and followed her inside.

"*Pon na ma?*" he asked.

"*Sí papisito, habla espanol?*"

"*Poquito.*" He smiled.

"*Chino, no?*" she said as she rolled down her top. Big brown torpedo nipples.

"*Sí,*" Lucky said, undressing. "*Chino.*"

They were naked on the mattress and she was licking him. He heard himself moaning, watching her tongue working him, then sucking him into Chinaman heaven.

"*Ma mao bicho,*" he whispered, *blow me,* holding her by the neck. He got rock hard and turned her over, entered the rich brown of her, doggie style.

"*Mi amor,*" she was whispering, his *lun* cock stroking her.

"*Mamita,*" he groaned like the low growl of a dog, and came long and angrily, deep inside of her.

Memory

As was her routine on Sunday afternoons, Mona pressed the Discman's plugs into her ears, adjusted the volume, then wrapped the Hermès silk square over her head and knotted it under her chin. Shirley Kwan sang a ballad into her brain as the elevator descended, and before Mona stepped out onto Henry Street, she slipped the black Vuarnets over her eyes.

She took the side streets south, away from the China Plaza, went as far as the Seaport and turned west toward the Hudson River. She didn't know the names of the streets but followed landmarks from memory, walking distance from Chinatown recalled. The way led through the steel-and-glass canyons of the Business District, pass a *gwailo* American department store where she found designer lingerie, toiletries, household items. Farther down that street was a travel agency she recognized by the pictures of ships and exotic locales, and a model airliner, displayed in the show window. On one occasion she had noticed a Chinese woman inside, wearing the red uniform blazer of the agency. *Lucky red*, she'd thought, and *jook-sing*, born American, she'd guessed.

Her route took her toward the river until she reached the World Financial Center. The promenade was deserted, as she had expected. She looked out over the harbor where the rivers met and mixed into riptides.

In the near distance she could see the Statue of Liberty, and she considered the word *freedom*, but remembered Uncle Four's bitter remarks about the exclusion of the Chinese, especially Chinese women, from these shores. She switched off the Discman, peered out beyond the choppy expanse of water, and began to wonder about *liberty*, and what she would need to do to gain it.

Out on the wet blue shining, the ships and boats reminded her of Hong Kong, *the fragrant harbor*, and as she stroked her piece of jade her mind reeled back to lost youth and forgotten hopes.

In Hong Kong she had crowded into cousins' bunk beds until she was sixteen, when she feared uncle would come into her room at night, herself the only girl there. She remembered wanting to be a movie star.

The memories that came after were mostly about jobs she had

had long before she'd managed to work her way up from Wanchai to Central, in Club Volvo, in TsimSha Cheui, the tourist sex ghetto, before she'd wound up on Nathan Road.

She'd worked component assembly at TongKai Precision, in the beauty-care industry, making devices called Beauty Facial Sauna, Eye Massager, Deep Heat Body Massager, Scalp Stimulator—touted to improve blood circulation, cleanse the skin, eliminate cellulite.

That position lasted six months, then Fat Louie Kai tried to stimulate her blood circulation against her will. She remembered working for *lo fei* Yat "Playboy" Pang, an aging gangster and the boss of Electronix Express, stamping circuit boards, LEDs, voice programs for talking thermo clocks: Mr. Temperature. Thermo-Talk Inc. The clocks presented multilingual digital displays and humanlike electronic voices that reported time and temperature in English, Spanish, French, German, Cyrillic, and Chinese (Mandarin only). Every hour, or at the touch of a button.

Every two months, databanks and calculators.

In the fall, children's programs for Christmas toys. Talking MathQuiz Pinball, Ring Back Talking Phone, Phone Calculator Pencil Box.

In one period, she assembled flashlights for five weeks.

In Chai Wan, she'd assembled plastics for High Speed Industries, snapping together pocket digital gambling games labeled Blackjack, Slot Machine, Craps, Roulette, Poker, Baccarat, and Deuces. Miniature versions were attached to keychains.

In Tseun Wan she had attached watchbands onto digital and quartz watches, in two months rising up the production line at Best Fortune Inc. to mini-alarm clocks and electronic pedometers.

Assembly work was all the same. Girls and women slouched

over their workstations under the fluorescent lights, sometimes twenty or thirty on each side of a long conveyor belt, working their goods onto the moving rubber blacktop. They were seated on backless stools, sometimes metal, sometimes plastic or cheap handcrafted bamboo.

The factories were unbearable in the humid monsoon season, a mindless drudgery always. She punched in just after the sun came up. Punched out when the moon put a bright hole against the deep blue of night.

Another time she'd been a sales rep for costume jewelry and accessories made in Mainland China and selling well at large department stores in Taiwan, Singapore, Thailand, and Japan. She never got used to hotels and airports. Tak Sing Imitation Jewelry. Necklaces, earrings, bangles, hair clasps. Gold- and silver-plated steel key rings, cufflinks. It didn't last.

A different man, a different product. Wholesale rep for Everrich Handbags factory. Portfolios, briefcases, clutches, purses, shoulder bags. Leather cowhide wallets, makeup cases, and organizers.

She learned quickly the play between sex and money. If sex was attached to the job, best to be paid richly for it. Seek men with power, wealth.

Always it was a man who provided a job, always a man who took it away. Always for the same reason: she wouldn't have sex with them. When the time came to fire her, it was because her work habits were unsatisfactory, or business was bad and layoffs were necessary. Or inventory turned up missing from her line.

Men. No sex. No job.

Seven jobs in two years. Along the way, dirty old men, nasty young men. Sun Tak thugs who fancied themselves playboys passed her around among themselves. Several European industrialists who had pledged their love until they'd bankrupted their businesses and abandoned her.

The longest job lasted nine months, at Fook Inc., the island's largest watchmaker, until old man Ah Fook died and young son Fook came around wanting what all the others before him demanded.

She'd moved on.

Now the sounds of the waterfront receded and she found herself following the traffic down the side streets back toward Chinatown.

Help

Tin Nee Beauty Salon was a beauty-and-fitness emporium on the second floor of the Jade Building, in the middle of the noise roaring along Canal Street. Exercise machines, whirlpool. Manicure.

Mona maintained a regular appointment every other Sunday, but she was later than usual on this afternoon. Facial, sauna. A massage, the purity of innocent hands rubbing, squeezing away the poisonous touch of a piggish old man. Steam and heat purging the smell of Uncle Four from her pores.

She sank her body into the massage table, remembering *Water Over Thunder, strengthen base of operations.*

But how?

If she could find a woman, an accomplice, to help her secure a false passport or a new identity, she might be able to escape. But who? The secrecy of her relationship to Uncle Four forbade her any ordinary friends. And she didn't trust women anyway, especially the gossipers who cut her hair and polished her nails, always slipping in rude questions she had to evade. They never said what they knew, although she suspected they knew enough to *gong sifay*— spread gossip—behind her back as soon as she stepped out of the salon. So she went to several salons during the year, rotating them, thinking she could keep them off balance.

But who? Working-class women, factory women, would be suspicious of her, would misjudge her intentions. The *siu lai lai*, socialites, would recognize her for what she was, *cheap see*, mistress, and would disdain her, betray her.

The counterfeit-identification business was underground traffic, and if she was betrayed, Uncle Four would surely punish her.

She pressed her fingers into the jade piece, her hand sweaty from the masseuse's artistry of pushing hands. Lake over water. *Trapped. Abandoned, alone, nowhere to turn.* Muscles loosening up. *Sign of Sacrifice. Insight matures, resolves swells.*

Help, she pleaded to herself.

Golo

Having dispatched the *dailo* to correct the gang boys wayward extortions at the far end of East Broadway, Golo Chuk, the once-feared Hip Ching enforcer, returned to his one-bedroom walk-up on Pell, tossed his pack of 555s onto the bed, and undressed. In the mirror behind the door he saw a forty-nine-year-old man, six-foot-two inches tall, bald except for the short hair graying at his temples. He looked like a waiter, an accountant, a clerk, certainly not like a Red Pole, enforcer rank, in the *Hung Huen*—Red Circle Triad.

He turned on the cable TV, kept the Chinese program low, just loud enough to add some noise to the empty space.

On the TV there was Hong Kong gunplay. He watched it from the corners of his eyes, and opened up the pack of cigarettes. He shook out an eighth of Chinese Number Three, a teak-brown powder in a glassine packet. The powder was flecked throughout with larger, rockier chunks. He pulled the foil from the cigarette pack, made a chute out of it and carefully extracted one of the tiny rocks between his fingers, handling it like *bow buey*, preciousness.

The little rock dropped onto the foil slide and he flicked his butane lighter under it. The grain gave off a vaporous trail that slowly made its way down the foil. Golo formed an "O" with his lips, following, inhaling the twisting, flowing trail of smoke. Shrinking as it went, the rock neared the end of the slide and he reversed it, until it was gone, all inside him. After a moment he said *chasing the dragon* so quietly it was almost like praying.

The Number Three was very uneven, lumpy, but better than ninety percent. Dark-skinned Hakkanese, fierce Hakka province drug runners, had told him the deal was three pounds, two kilos split in separate bricks, one-hundred-seventy-five thousand whole-sale. A steal.

Uncle Four pledged a hundred thousand cash along with the warning, *The price is too low but perhaps they are desperate for money. Doesn't sound like the Hakkas. They are trying to unload it for someone else, who has no distribution. Perhaps it is hijacked powder?*

Golo had talked the Hakkas into accepting the balance in gold Panda coins and diamonds stolen out of TsimSha Cheui in Hong Kong by the Red Circle Triad and on consignment at the Sun Fung. At a discount, of course.

Fifty one-ounce Pandas. Two dozen diamonds, a carat each of excellent cut and clarity.

The Hakka can wash gold and diamonds better than anybody.

Golo saw it very clearly: the Triad fronting the gold and ice, Uncle Four squaring the cash end, the Number Three going to the Dragons inside the welfare projects.

He fired up a 555. Reaching under the sofa bed, he came up with a gray-metal box with a combination dial. He sat on the bed and opened it, sucking down the cigarette. What came out of the box was a big glass jar, and a Chinese pistol. When he removed the gun, the banner of the *Hung Huen*, unfurled red Chinese characters on black cloth across the linoleum floor. Slogans. Myths. From their original, long-ago resolve to restore the Ming dynasty, honor had given way to greed, power, and bloodlust.

Cleaning it now, the gun felt heavy to the touch. It was a Tokarev M213, a nine-millimeter Parabellum of Chinese military issue, copied from the Russians. It had a thirteen-shot magazine and black rubber grips with a red star inset. He ran an oilcloth over the forged steel and stared at the glass jar.

In the glass jar was a severed hand, the hand of a *wing chun*— kung fu–style enforcer, tailing off into umbilicals of tendon and ligament, a shaft of bone protruding from the bloated and whitened flesh where the wrist ended and sure agony began.

Now, with the Number Three roiling his brain, he turned the jar slowly, held it up to the window's brightness. In the hard daylight, he could see with vivid clarity the details of the hand, its nails, fingerprints, fine lines, creases of the palm, calluses where the skin was thick, scarred and bunched around the knuckles, floating in the fluid formaldehyde from Wah San Funeral Home, rotating ever so slowly to accommodate his scrutiny.

Was it the heroin, or the memory of severing the hand that aroused such ferocious clarity, he wondered, putting out the cigarette. He muted the sound on the television. Leaning back on the bed, his head floated, and one of the blood oaths came back to him. *I shall be killed by myriads of swords if I embezzle cash or properties from my brethren.*

He put down the glass jar, glanced at the TV screen, then dipped a bore brush in and out of the heavy metal gun barrel, stroked it. He pulled back the slide and heard it *chik-cock* in place, then blew at it and released the slide, the crack of metal snapping back the action. When he squeezed the trigger the hammer dropped, chopping down with a hard *bock*.

And then he closed his eyes and filled his head with visions of diamonds and gold.

Hope

Mona wore a short bouclé jacket that was blacker than the lace bustier from Victoria's Secret underneath her open silk blouse, a modest black miniskirt, and suede Sesto Meucci pumps with chunky heels.

Johnny held the car door open for her and helped her in, her free hand holding the little flat Armani clutch that contained her makeup and keys. She squeezed his hand, and he closed the door after her.

They headed up the highway toward Yonkers Raceway to meet Uncle Four at the late races, the trotters. It was a half-hour drive up to White Plains, where Uncle Four hosted a delegation of Hip Chings from various cities along the East Coast, who had rented a slew of motel rooms across from the track.

"How are your business plans coming along?" she asked.

Johnny said he was still raising capital but was considering various schemes with some of the other drivers.

"I know people," she said, "who have money to *invest*." That caught his attention and he watched her in the rearview mirror as she lit up a cigarette. "Maybe you can get a partner, do better for yourself."

He listened.

"You don't want to drive me around forever, do you?" she asked.

She touched the back of his neck and he turned slightly and kissed her fingers, keeping his eyes on the highway. Reaching across to the dash, he turned on the cassette player and they sang Hong Kong love ballads together, like karaoke.

Then the cassette came to a sad song and she asked him to turn it off, casting them into an uneasy silence.

"I have need of a gun," she said suddenly, softly but clearly. "There are men who come around the building. They go through the garbage cans and sometimes chase me for money."

He never flinched. "What kind of gun?" he asked.

"A small gun, something I can carry in my bag."

The face of fat Tony Biondo, the only *gwai lo* Johnny knew, came into his mind.

"Money's no problem. I need something I can rely on."

Johnny nodded, *mo mun tay*, no problem.

"A gun with one of those things that keep it quiet." In the rearview, Mona saw his eyes go curious.

"If I need to use it," she added quickly, "the less attention the better."

Their eyes locked a moment.

"Immigration," she said quietly.

Johnny understood, said he'd see what was available, get her a price.

"I knew I could trust you," Mona said with a sad smile.

They arrived at Yonkers and she went to Uncle Four's side. *Like a pet cat,* Johnny thought, *a black cat crossing his path.* The members of the delegation came out of Boston, Philadelphia, Miami, and Washington, and they all brought whores, or shared whores.

The whores were all colors and tried to pass themselves off as "models" and "escorts."

Johnny left them and went down to the other end of the track. He had two more hours to dust, didn't want to watch Mona, and the wad he'd won at Belmont was scorching his pockets.

He copped a racing form, and looked for more angles to play, to take his mind off of Mona.

Past And Present

The last thing he had heard was the radio.

Then it became the first thing he heard, tinny music chasing him through the night back to Chinatown with Billy's folded cardboard boxes, ready to pack up Pa's stuff.

Jack wolfed down forkfuls of rice and *cheng dao* from a gravy of ground beef and bits of fried-egg yellow that clung to the side of the splayed takeout container. He scanned Pa's apartment and took inventory more with his heart than with his eyes.

When he was full he went to the black knapsack and took out one of the disposable InstaFlash cameras. He set the black gourd-shaped bottle down on Pa's table, thumbed open the cap and poured a big splash into a beer glass and took a swallow. The mao-tai was 150-proof rice liquor, more fiery than the Johnny Black he was used to, and left a bitter aftertaste following the scorch down his throat. Damn, he cursed on an incendiary breath, screwing his eyes tight. Moving about the dim apartment, he flashed off the thirty-six shots of the throwaway.

He took another swallow so he could begin to forget the way things looked.

Cans and bottles he placed together, along with dried goods and herbal medicines, in a box for the Old Age Center, to go along with the television, the kitchen appliances.

Pa's old clothes lay neatly stacked on his bed, bound for the Salvation Army instead of the Senior Citizens, since none of the old Chinamen would wear the clothes of the deceased.

The furniture, books, and household artifacts would be split between the Women's Shelter, and the Chinatown History Project.

He poured another splash.

In the last box he placed the things he needed to keep: citizenship papers, a bank account held in trust under his name containing five thousand dollars. A steamship ticket forty years old, Ma's passage to America. A copy of his own birth certificate, St. Vincent's Hospital, 1965.

Behind the dusty *kwan kung*, God of War figurine, with the urn of burnt-out incense, he found two more photographs, so evenly layered with dust that he knew they hadn't been touched in many years. In one he wore a crewcut and a paratrooper's uniform, no smile on his face. The other was a graduation picture taken at the Police Academy, a blue peaked cap over his eyes.

He stared at the photos, and ran his tongue but could not wet the dryness from his lips.

"*Chaai lo ah?* Now you're a cop?" Pa had said through teeth clenched in derision. "First it was the army, *dong bing*, enlisting. You thought they would accept you? Die for a country that hates you?"

Jack had stood silent, had heard the argument before it reached his ears.

"Chinese don't become policemen. They're worse than the crooks. Everyone knows they take money. *Nei cheega*, you're crazy, you have lost your *jook-sing*—American born—mind. I didn't raise you to be a *kai dai*—punk idiot—so they could use you against your own people."

He became a cop anyway, a ticket out of Chinatown.

And they did use me against my own people, but only against the bad ones, and I never took any money. Words he'd never found the chance to say to Pa.

Jack dropped the photographs into the box, the rice liquor working heavy on his eyelids. He stacked the boxes in the middle of the room, returned to the gourd bottle.

Cops didn't get paid for the blazing shootouts and death-defying car chases that were commonplace on TV. By and large, the average cop clocked in his years and put in for a pension, never having fired a round, his service piece never clearing its holster.

Cops were paid to sop up images of body bags and toe tags, to record the horrific ugliness of butchered corpses and grisly executions, to clean up the bloody mess daily, like a sponge, so that the suits and the white collars wouldn't have to sully their psyches, or get their fingernails dirty.

Cops had to look for justice in quiet and painstaking investigations after the fact, and more often than not, they came up empty.

There was a morgue of unsolved cases larger than the public library.

He did four cop years the hard way, plainclothes duty in the South Bronx, then Harlem, East New York, and Sunset Park, before he returned to the Chinatown stationhouse. Now he wasn't sure Detective One was in his future, and making sergeant even less likely. Plus he'd seen enough dead and brutalized bodies to start wondering if being a cop was the right answer. Maybe there were other possibilities in life, short as it is. Or else, he could hang in there and wind up eating the gun. Did he make a difference? The way things happened in Chinatown, he didn't feel like he did. Always a lot of questions that didn't come up with answers.

The mao-tai flamed down his throat.

There were scattered items on the card table Pa used as a desk. A Hong Kong ashtray. There was a small *kwan kung* statuette next to a framed, faded color photograph of a threesome: Pa and Ma much younger, and he, Jack the baby, in the middle. They were in a park somewhere, wearing summer clothes.

Grandpa had been a laundryman, but he managed to serve in World War II, and was able to bring his China son, Pa, then eleven, to America through the War Brides Act.

Grandma had chosen to return to China.

The rest was foggy.

Two decades later, Ma would be dead, buried in the village of her sisters, in the south of China, where she'd gone to visit but had contracted cholera and died. Pa had been stunned. He took it as a sign, tried to raise the boy himself.

Jack remembered grammar school. They had Parent-Teacher Days but Pa always worked, never attended. The other kids called Jack *gwoo yee*, orphan.

Jack capped the gourd, went over to the bed. *Granpa went home to Toishan. Pa got the Laundry. Ma died.*

And like most of his Chinamen brethren, Pa never believed in life insurance. "*Dai ga lai see,*" he'd say. "Don't ask for bad luck."

He'd had no Social Security, no nest egg. Money never figured in the sum of his life.

Yu gor, brother Yu, the laundrymen had called Pa; he had the biggest heart, big with the giving of his all. Until the giving ran out, when it stopped beating one sudden dark morning, and the old sojourner's wandering was abruptly canceled, betrayed by the heart he'd given of so generously. Not to burden his son, he'd left six thousand in cash; a grimy stack of hundred-dollar bills in a safe-deposit box at the Bank of China. It paid for the pre-arranged funeral expenses, allowed him to depart with face and leave no shame for his son.

For that son, there was a hundred-dollar savings bond, and a note on folded white paper which contained his final message. When Jack had Pa's note translated, it read: *I have seen that long shadow behind me, that shadow of our many ancestors. You, my son, are part of that unseen shadow that precedes me, the shadow of my descendants. There is no grandchild, no great-grandchild that I can see. That shadow ends with you. Yet you have the responsibility to make that shadow as long as the one behind me, though I may not live to see it. Remember where you came from. Know who you are. Know where you are going.*

This, thought Jack, from a man who believed only in the struggle of the laundrymen, who fought for his kindred brothers, workingmen all, slaves to the eight-pound steam iron.

The tragedy of the laundrymen, recalled Jack. *Could they have known where they were going? Hemmed in by racism? Made unnecessary by the age of machines?* He had played his fingers over the crispness of the savings bond, speechless in the silence of the private room in the basement of the bank where he'd opened his father's safety deposit box, the silence of things left unfinished, feelings left unspoken. Now it was too late. The bad feelings between father and son were left unresolved. Pa, dying alone. At the end, had there been forgiveness or recrimination?

Jack would never know, but just wanted to say once what in life he'd been too angry and stubborn to admit. *I did love you, Father, after all.*

The memories ached inside him, undiminished by alcohol. He checked his watch against the darkness outside Pa's window, and remembered Billy, and the midnight meet at Grandpa's.

Struggle

The Golden Star Bar and Grill, known locally as Grandpa's, was a wide basement window three steps down from the street with a video game by the front and a pool table in the back. The bar was a long wraparound oval under shadowy blue light, which ran along the perimeter of the ceiling, obscuring a mixed-bag clientele colored more Lower Eastside than Chinatown. A few Chinese. White. Puerto Rican. Black.

Jack set up a nine-ball rack snugly and tossed the wooden triangle under the pool table. It was eleven p.m., Wilson Pickett doing "Midnight Hour" on the jukebox. Jack hit on a beer, then stroked the stick back and out in a fluid, piston motion, until it felt right, then slammed the tip high on the cue ball, blasting it toward the triangle-shaped cluster of nine balls.

The cluster broke with a sharp crack, scattering the balls, the white cue ball following hard through them. Jack studied the layout of balls. Billy had said midnight so there was time to chase a couple of racks around the green-felt table.

He knew he wasn't good enough to run nine balls unless the

rack opened up exactly the right way, keeping the shots simple for him. Rarely happened. *Divide and conquer,* he was thinking, *Sun Tsu. Split the rack. Try hard to run four or five balls, then repeat, a second run of four or five.*

Nothing had gone down, the colored balls settling across the middle of the table. The one, two, three, he could make those. The four and five split out toward the end pockets, he'd have to work for those. He scraped the blue chalk cube across the tip of his stick and sighted the two, then drew back on the one, watched it drop as the white ball rolled behind the two. Straight shot, side pocket, followed by the three. He hit the beer, chalked again, scanned the place for Billy. Left-side English on the three spun the cue ball off the side rail toward the far end. Four ball, five, at the end of the table. He drew low and hard. The four went down with a plop, the cue ball skidding toward the other end, positioning off to the right. A cut shot, tight and thin.

He missed the five, took a long swallow of beer. Didn't see Billy. He followed through the rest of the rack until the nine ball dropped, and Billy walked into the bar.

They took a booth in the back and ordered a round of boilermakers, huddled together in cigarette smoke.

"The boys in the shop," Billy said, "think the rapist comes from outside of Chinatown, outside the city, on his day off. Works in a restaurant or factory, upstate maybe, where there's no Chinese around. Takes the bus down to the city."

They gulped liquor and Jack listened.

"The guy probably has a rent-a-bed in the area."

"Fukienese?"

"Probably, but don't get me wrong. Most of them are hardworking people, like slaves. Until they pay back their passage, they have to live under the gun, know what I'm saying?" He ordered more shots.

"Farrakhan," he grimaced, "comes on the TV and calls them *bloodsuckers.* Colin Ferguson gets on the Long Island Railroad and blows away two Asian women and the Nation of Islam praises him."

The shots came and they touched glasses like it was a declaration of war.

"Black gangbangers loot and burn the Koreans out of L.A. and the cops, man, they cut and run. No one cares."

Jack shrugged. "It's different now. You get killed for looking at someone the wrong way. For stepping on someone's shoe. *Dissing,* they call it. The rapper's rap it and the movies blow it up bigger than life."

Billy tapped the rim of the beer glass.

"It's open season on Chinamen."

Jack watched him drain it, his eyes telling the truth. *Chinese people never enslaved Black people, never robbed or lynched them. The Black Rage angle had nothing to do with the Chinese, who suffered under the same weight of discrimination as the Blacks did. The Black-on-Yellow crime wave was blind racist hate, straight up and simple.*

"You know how it works, Jack. White cop shoots a black kid, the niggers riot, loot the Asian merchants." He signaled for another shot.

"Ease up," Jack said. "We got time yet."

There was a sigh, a disdainful shake of the head from Billy before he spoke again.

"Yeah. The other thing you asked about. The muscle behind the snakehead human traffickers? Yo, the Fuk *Ching* are the young guns down East Broadway, but the Fuk *Chow* have a lot of older guys, in their thirties and forties. Most of them are ex-People's Army. They got military training. *Thems* the ones you've got to look out for. The young Chings got Tech-nines and Magnums, but the old grunts got Chinese Makarovs and AK-47s. Explosives, too, know what I'm saying? What happened in Fort Lee was strictly hothead stuff. Revenge. You ain't seen nothing yet. Wait till they really set up their numbers."

Jack shook his head, crushed his cigarette.

"A lotta shit," Billy said. "And you're eyebrow deep, pal. The badge that heavy on you?"

"I'm in a different position now, Billy."

"That badge don't make you any less a Chinaman, Jacky. Do what you got to do, but remember, you still just like me, like the rest of us. You don't have to go too far in NYC before someone reminds you who you are. We be *Chinamen,* Jack. You can't be happy till you accept what you are."

"I don't like boxing myself in like that."

"You kidding, right? You're a homeboy cop working Chinatown. You don't think you're boxed in?"

"I *asked* for the transfer back, Billy. The old man got sick. It was a hardship thing." Jack finished the beer. Billy shook his head.

"You know Chinatown well as me. Not for nothing, but you think the merchants are gonna stop giving it up because you came on the scene?"

"The merchants think it's easier to pay them off," Jack said.

"Nah, that's not it. They pay off because they know the cops can't protect them. Homeboy, you think you make a difference here?"

Jack didn't answer, but the waitress brought another round and when they toasted, Billy sprinkled whiskey onto the wooden floor.

"Your father was a standup guy, Jack. All the old-timers used to say so. He stood up for the laundrymen against the big laundromats. He challenged the City's labor taxes."

"That was a long time ago," Jack said, "and I wasn't around."

"They tried to make him out a commie, a troublemaker. But he had support in the community."

Jack remembered vague fragments as Billy went on.

"All that anti-American stuff he spoke, you never did believe it, did you?"

Jack finished his JB, shook his head slowly from side to side.

"I knew," Billy said. "You were proud to be American. That's why you joined the army. Not to get away from him, and Chinatown. Not because you hated what your father struggled for."

"Struggle," Jack agreed, "is a good word for it. There was a lotta years of that. Pa didn't understand. He thought I was nuts, or suicidal, or maybe I wanted to spite him by jumping out of airplanes."

"What happened with that?"

"I broke my ankle two weeks into Airborne out of Fort Benning. I went into Computer-Tech after that, but a year later they decided Computers was overloaded and I volunteered out. Two years, I did."

There was a silence that brought the jukebox music back between them, until Billy rapped his knuckles against the wooden bar, and spoke like he was seeing a warm summer memory.

"Whatever happened to that foxy Chinese babe you used to hang with? The one used to live on Mulberry, with the crazy mother?"

It was just Billy's way of changing the conversation, Jack knew, but the question made bittersweet the grief he was already feeling, and though he didn't have a choice, feeling sad or mad, he decided he didn't want either, settling for more whiskey and oblivion instead. Zero feeling, he knew, was better than bad feeling, better than searching for answers that never came.

Still, the question caught him off guard. He remained silent, his eyes searching the dim blue-lit room for an answer to something he'd allowed himself to forget, something he'd felt long ago, when women seemed more important, and love was full of possibilities.

Maylee. At eighteen, his Chinatown beauty queen.

He hadn't thought of her in the eight years since college, before he'd dropped out, before the Tofu King, before the army, and the NYPD.

Maylee. His first love, and first heartbreak. It taught him to dull his expectations, to be cautious with the giving of his heart.

The memory was a rush. Three tenements apart, they'd made love every day that long summer after high school, before college, except for the days she cramped, and then he'd pamper her, head to foot. Their love ended when the fall semester began, bringing college boys with BMWs cruising the campuses like matriculated hustlers.

Maylee noticed. She'd long wanted out of the dilapidated tenement, away from summer streets that stank raw with spoiled seafood, rotten fruit, restaurant garbage, overrun by rats and vermin. She was ashamed of how they lived, embarrassed by poverty and the narrow-mindedness of her culture.

Jack Yu, the boy next door, was sweet, but he wasn't the way out.

Her mother wasn't crazy, just afraid. Afraid her daughter would join the street gangs. Afraid she'd drop out of school, take up with a *gwailo*, a blue-eyed white devil. Afraid she'd get pregnant. Afraid she'd lose her Chineseness, forget her name, where she came from.

Afraid, afraid, afraid.

Afraid of all the things *lo fan*—foreigner—white, and American that her daughter desired to be, until finally that mother's fear drove the daughter away, but not until she had broken Jack's heart and made him want to leave also.

Maylee enrolled at Barnard. Jack squeezed into City College. Their classrooms just a mile of city streets apart, but their worlds already tumbling in opposite directions: she, edging her way uptown; he, falling back into Chinatown. It was Maylee who made him wary, but it was Wing's murder that made him hard-hearted, that erected the great wall around his emotions that protected him, isolated him.

"She cut loose, Billy. Got sick of Chinatown, married a *lo fan* white boy, moved to Connecticut. Became a lawyer, or doctor," Jack heard his whiskey voice answering, ice cubes clinking the glass in his hand.

"Haven't seen her in years," he said carelessly, drinking away the contradictions in his private life, gaining short bursts of clarity in the alcoholic reaching for oblivion. Halfway gone, only then was he able to make some sense of it all.

After Maylee, there came a series of unrewarding, unsatisfying affairs, with Asian girls he'd figured he had something in common with, affairs ultimately overshadowed by the differences in their cultural attitudes. The Japanese considered themselves superior to the Chinese. The Chinese never forgot the Japanese atrocities in World War Two. Koreans were clannish, rude, spiteful in the face of Eastern history, their occupation by the Japs. Vietnamese and Cambodians never got over China's part in their wars of liberation. Indians, Filipinos, Thais, their skin was too dark. Poverty and colonialism settled their place in the Asian pecking order. Later generations paying for the crimes and weaknesses of their ancestors. Attitudes steeped in centuries of struggle, prejudice and pride, too strong for Jack's brief Americanization to overcome. He knew who he was, but refused to let history trap him the way it did Pa. In New York, in the last decade of the twentieth century, love had become too complex, sex too risky, intimacy too great a compromise. Jack let it go, found his own center, decided to let love flow to him, instead of him chasing after it. Patience, Pa would have said, was a virtue. The right one would come along. Later, there were Puerto Rican women, and artistic women of color from the Village, but never white women, to whom he was invisible, the Chinaman no man. Sure, he thought, had he been wealthy, or possessed a fancy car back then, it might have made a difference. Money transcended color. Class transcended race.

In that equation, he'd known that women had all the power. Asian women could sell out, cop to the plea, give up the struggle, because they were desired. Asian men had to live with their struggles for acceptance. In his mind it sounded bitter. It felt the same.

He ordered another round and they watched Grandpa's fill up with radio car drivers and their raucous passengers of the night. Pretty ladies and gangsters. Gato Barbieri wailed out of the jukebox and when they finished their drinks, Jack left Billy at the bar, each of them feeling sadder and more alone.

Karaoke

The Sing Along Song Club was a walk-up assembly-hall space in the White Tiger Crane Kung Fu Academy. The school was operated by the Hip Chings on weekdays only. The hall was recast as the Sing Along from nine at night until three a.m. every night of the week.

Young men from the Association came each night and rolled

out the tables, laid on the tablecloths and topped them with candles. Liquor was inside locked wall cabinets that folded out into a display shelf behind a long, low wooden bar, with red-topped barstools that the students sat on during Kung Fu practice. The other long wall was lined with mirrors.

It was a turnkey disco-ball operation. Hit a switch, dim the lights. The huge flat-screen projection TV lit up the back wall. Pin spots of light spun off the mirrored ball. The Samsung CD-OK laser karaoke machine kicked in. Pick up a microphone and follow the bouncing ball.

Every half hour, smoke rolled in from the Fogmaker 200, and they punched up the audio. The girls in black mini-dresses came out with trays of Remy XO cognac and served them at the covered tables.

Dragons were posted near the doors, and they screened for weapons.

The place usually opened with Hong Kong college students and got cooking after midnight when the hardcore older crowd came in from the gambling joints, the tracks, the late action at OTB. The *siu jeer*, young lady hostesses, arrived at twelve-thirty and picked off the single men.

The CD-OK machine had a capacity of fifteen thousand songs and videos in a single compact disk, and featured auto-mike mixing and echo for giving the singer a pro sound even after a fifth of XO.

The cognac had been stolen from Chin Wah Distributors, twelve bottles a case, twenty-five cases in all. A twenty-five-thousand dollar score by the Dragons, more when the girls served it out at a hundred-fifty each fifth. Counting the five-dollar cover, they cleared a thousand a night, easy. *Not* counting the fifty-dollar bags of Jamaican, the hundred-dollar glassines of Chinese Number Three, *balown sooga*.

The Sing Along had contest nights during which the collegiate Hong Kong wannabees partied hearty. Toward the Double Ten parties, celebrating the anniversary of the founding of the Republic of China on October tenth, more people crushed in from out of town, hungry for the action, and the Association gladly fed the volatile mix.

It was past midnight.

Johnny watched Mona follow Uncle Four up the flight of stairs into the Sing Along. He had been told to return in an hour, and was considering what to do with the hundred dollars he had left after his losing streak at Yonkers.

He decided he was hungry and went for a quick *siew yeh* at the Harmonious Garden. The chef boiled him up some noodles and chopped in pieces of soy-sauce chicken and roast pork. There was a *Hong Kong Star* magazine for him to read and after that there wasn't enough time to go to Fat Lily's so he went back to the Sing Along and waited.

The karaoke game wasn't for old men. They sat around smoking cigars and drinking cognac, watching thirty-year-old ladies chirp wistfully about better times and romances lost and found.

It was only the second visit for Mona, the Sing Along not being one of her favorite places. Too many gang kids and *hom sup*, horny, Chinatown men. Still, she sat in her place beside Uncle Four, who had met up with Golo Chuk, the three of them at a table beside the mirrored wall. She glanced at her reflection in the candlelight and noticed the group of men at the next table, smiling, making eyes at her. She flashed her eyes, then ignored them. The club was crowded and the hostesses were working the room, but there weren't enough of them to go around.

The men were Taiwanese, Mona judged by their accents,

banker types, from their suits and ties. They were working on their second fifth of XO and smoking up a storm cloud.

Golo picked up on them, figured them as *bok los*, northern Chinese, slumming for southern Cantonese snatch.

"*Shau mei*," one of the bankers said across the tables. "Don't you remember me?"

Uncle Four and Mona exchanged looks, hers saying, *He's mistaken, I don't know them.*

Golo thought, *How dare they insult us in our own place!*

"*Ta ma da*," he said in his best cutting Mandarin. "What the fuck are you looking at?"

That started it.

Two of the suits closest to Golo stood up as he pushed back from the table. In a single motion, Golo kicked out one man's kneecap, and driving his *hung kuen*, red-style fist, full force, split open the other man's face. Glass tumblers flew across and crashed into the mirrored wall, shattering onto Uncle Four and Mona.

Suddenly, the Sing Along was in pandemonium, emptying out as the Black Dragons beat the hell out of the Taiwanese, trying to cool out Golo Chuk.

The pin spots of light kept whirling and the song machine kept wailing even as the Dragons dragged the bloody men across the empty hall.

Fear

Johnny flung down the racing form as people dashed out of the Sing Along. He jumped out of the car just in time to hold the door for Mona and Uncle Four.

"What happened?" he asked once they were inside the car.

"A fight," huffed Uncle Four. "*Faan ukkei,* get home."

Johnny wasn't sure which home Uncle Four meant but started the car. He looked in the rearview and saw fear in Mona's eyes.

"Henry *gaai,*" she said coolly, and he turned the car toward the Henry Street condo. It was a short drive, and he could feel the heat of Uncle Four's anger curling the short hairs on the back of his neck.

Quickly enough he was there, watching as Uncle Four marched Mona into the China Plaza, her heels clicking along the stone lobby floor, clutching the little purse to her bosom.

When they were out of sight, he doused the headlights and killed the engine. He felt helpless, and stayed in the car until the lights on her balcony came on. When the light went instantly to black, he fired up the car, and thought about Fat Lily's.

But his pockets were empty, and he wheeled the limo around, looking toward his home.

It was bad enough when Uncle Four drank too much cognac, but now he was in a simmering rage.

He grabbed Mona, then shoved, tearing the silk of her blouse, ripping it off along with the black lacy bra. He slapped her across the face, which he never did, not wanting the bruises to show, but this time leaving a dull pink palm print, and sprinkling bloody spittle from her mouth. Shoving her onto the bed, he grabbed her by the hair, slapped at the back of her head.

She knew not to resist, or be defiant. It would only enrage him further. *Play along, suffer it.* He'd be more forgiving in a day or two, and then it'd be flowers and champagne.

He unbuckled his belt and slipped it off the loops, whipped her with it across the buttocks.

"I cannot face you," Mona sobbed. "I won't dare next time. Please forgive me," she whimpered, choking on her words.

At this, he tossed the belt aside, stripped her skirt and panties off and turned her over. He dropped his trousers and forced her legs apart.

She cried out and he shoved her face into the pillows, plowing into her. *Kuan Yin, Goddess of Mercy,* she was thinking, *have mercy on me,* as Uncle Four vented his hatred hard inside her.

Cop

Daylight came again, made stark those things that had blended in with night and artificial light. The alarm on Jack's watch jingled. He barely noticed it and took five minutes to roll off Pa's bed of clothes. He went to the green-streaked sink to splash water on his face. It was too late for breakfast and too early for roll call at the 0-Five. But he'd had enough of the dead air and the dark night. From the knapsack he extracted the cellular phone, the pager, another disposable InstaFlash. He opened all the windows before he left the apartment, the cool morning breeze at his back as his feet pounded the stairs until he stepped onto Mott Street and into the roar of the morning.

The tension was building. He could feel it pulling, grabbing inside his shoulders.

When he entered the stationhouse he passed an old Chinese woman seated at one of the benches, bleeding from the mouth, her eyes glazing over from the shock, a broken half circle of jade bracelet in her hand.

P.O. Jamal Josephs, a.k.a. Jay Jay, brushed past Jack with a wet paper towel and gave it brusquely to the old woman. Turning, he threw a pissed-off look in Jack's direction.

Jamal was a leading member of the Ebony Guards, a black fraternal police organization that had success nullifying sergeants' examinations based on charges of discrimination and cheating. Recently, thirteen thousand cops had been tested and five hundred made sergeant. The Guards alleged widespread cheating among white cops and filed suit against the City for allowing the exam to be compromised. The Department of Investigation was figuring out how many, if any, of the five hundred had prior access to the exams.

When Jay Jay came back he leaned into Jack, jerking his two fingers back at the old woman, saying, "She keeps flashing me the peace sign, Yu. '*Hock-kwee, hock-kwee*,' she keeps saying, and I *know* what it means, Jack. I know what it means and I don't need it, okay?"

Jack said, "What does it mean, Josephs?" He walked over to the old woman without waiting for Jay Jay's answer, sat down opposite her and spoke quietly in Toishanese, watching the look on her face go from surprise back to fear, to resignation, telling her story.

When she finished, Jack came back from the bench. Jay Jay, waiting with crossed arms, said with a challenge, "*Hock-kwee* means black devil. It means *nigger,* right?" Jack was silent looking from Josephs back to the old woman.

Jay Jay said, "See, Jack, I know what it means and don't need it, know what I'm sayin'?"

Jack leaned in closer, said into Josephs' eyes, "That's right, Josephs, you don't like it but there it is. It wasn't the peace sign, man, it was *two,* like in two black *African-American soul brothers* from the Smith Houses mugging a seventy-year-old Chinese

97

grandmother, busting out her dentures, but all you can hear is *nigger,* right?"

"Fuck that racist shit," Jay Jay said in a low growl.

"Yeah, fuck it," Jack answered, "'cause half the fuckin crime in the Projects is committed against Asians by blacks, and what's *racist* about it is that you can't face up to it, how badly you're fucking up as a people."

Sergeant Paddy *Staten-Island-Irish* Murphy got his considerable girth between them.

"Be nice, boys," he huffed. "Don't want to spoil the captain's morning, do we?"

"Fuck you, Jack," Jay Jay, a.k.a. P.O. Josephs said, backing away.

"Likewise, *brother.*" Jack watched Josephs storm off, knew that was the way it was in this precinct, this city, this country.

The white cops resented the black cops for the breaks they got on the examinations, saw them as quota promotions, affirmative-action freeloaders. Male cops disliked female officers. Black and Latino cops resented the few Asian cops who were advanced on the coattails of *their* struggle, ignoring that the yellows were academically better prepared.

Jack wasn't one of them. Any of *them.* He was becoming the loner in his professional life that he was in his personal life. So *they* couldn't figure him out; the inscrutable Oriental, Detective Charlie Chan, they joked behind his back.

The NYPD didn't possess any more sanctity than the rest of the city. If indeed the force was a mirror of society, then racism and sexism had to be a part of the reflection, the culture of violence and racism going hand in hand, as American as a Colt .45.

The highest ranking Chinese was a captain in the 0-Seven, a hometown boy who grew up on the Lower East Side, whose promotion no doubt chafed more than a few rednecks from Staten

Island to the Bronx. The old veterans didn't care for the shine of Chinese brass. It blinded them from seeing the bigger picture of a cop's duty: to protect, to *serve*.

Sergeant Murphy took Jack over to the locker room.

"Don't let 'im bug ya, Jacky boy," he said. "He's so fulla shit it's gushing out his fingernails. That's why he got bounced out the Three-Four and the Nine-Seven. 'Tween you an me, the niggers can't hold a candle to the Chinamen." He grinned.

Jack's anger flushed, spread sideways.

"Yeah, Paddy," Jack said, pulling away, "you know it. My father and grandfather waited tables full of good laddies like yourself. And did your laundry, too. They didn't like you, but they never spit in your food, or cursed about the small change you left on the tables. They could have, but they never did. They just went about their business. Them good *Chinamen*, Paddy."

Murphy stood there speechless, the red rising in his cheeks.

Jack turned and went up the stairs, the tension at the back of his head now.

Back to work, his mind was telling him, *let the work clear out the funk of Pa's passing*. His anger had been vented, and he channeled what remained of the adreno-rush toward the open-case files on the desk.

He took three breaths, centered himself, focused. The thinnest file was the most recent, labeled Chinatown Rapist using the headline slug from the *Daily News*. The report said that a slender Asian man in his twenties was raping young Chinese girls on the Lower East Side. Detectives from the Sex Crimes unit had officially taken over and composite sketches had gone out, and were posted throughout the Fifth and the Seventh Precincts, in apartment buildings, *gung chongs*—factories—bodegas, on corner lampposts. By-the-book procedure.

A week after the headlines, he'd struck again. A six-year-old Taiwanese girl this time. Forced her to the roof at knifepoint and sodomized her. *Right back into the neighborhood, snatched another one right under their noses.*

They had semen samples and Chinatown rumors. *The Fukienese, the new ones, it must be them. One of the boat slaves. Who else could go so low but the Fuk Chow?*

The Benevolent Associations respectfully pressured the police for action. The families of the victims secretly met with their tongs.

Now, there was only the waiting.

Jack went from the file to the night-shift blotter on the wall behind him. There was a notation after the shift changed that four Chinese men had been admitted to Emergency at Downtown Hospital with nonlethal gunshot wounds. All were Fukienese, and all claimed to be victims of a drive-by shooting by perpetrators unknown. Beat cops at the alleged shooting location found no evidence of any shooting.

Somebody's lying about something, Jack thought immediately, to cover up something bigger. For a moment his mind drifted, then he caught himself. The night dicks. Their shift, and they'd caught the squeal. He'd be wasting his time.

He went back to the files.

The last file, which he'd titled Fuk Ching/Golden Venture, was thick with photographs and news articles.

Ten Chinamen had drowned in the rough and frigid chop as hundreds more jumped ship. The reports had crackled back and forth on the Fury's radio. The Coast Guard plucked up the dead bodies, rounded up the shivering human cargo for Immigration. They were counted, declared a *menace*, shuffled onto buses for detention, escorted by a flotilla of police wearing surgical masks.

The backlash began almost immediately. The media painted them ugly, called them "human contraband," "economic refugees," the new Yellow Peril, coming to take American jobs, to take food out of the mouths of American children. The *New York Post* declared *Thousands Feared in NY Dungeons*, dragging up the Ghost of Fu Manchu, and illegal alien *slaves* kept prisoner by Chinese *se jai*, snakehead, gangsters. The tag "Snakeheads" was added to the American vocabulary.

At City Hall, the first black mayor said nothing. No black voices rose up to decry the new slave trade.

One ship a week, seven hundred workers per, thirty thousand a head. Twenty million per shipload. It wasn't the first time Chinese people jumped ship. Grandpa had done it several times in the Forties. America didn't want the Chinese then, didn't want them now.

Never had a Chinamen's chance, thought Jack, frowning at the irony.

He scanned the most recent report describing gunfire blasting the pre-dawn quiet over Teaneck, a sleepy New Jersey town near the Hackensack River. The state troopers had arrived at the rented Fuk Ching safehouse and found the bodies.

On the first floor, two Chinese men lay dead of knife and gunshot wounds. In the basement, two others, bound with duct tape, shot in the head point-blank. Outside the house, another wounded man, DOA at Hackensack Medical.

A Chinatown gang war had spilled across the river.

Stuck to the case file was a square of yellow memo on which he had written *Alexandra Lee-Chow, AJA, 10 a.m.*

The methods of the flesh smugglers had morphed, and suddenly Chinese boat people were detained in Honolulu, Southern California, San Francisco Bay, San Diego Harbor, Jacksonville

Bay, and as close as Baltimore, and Charlotte. Now they had arrived in New York City, crashing only because a violent rift between the Fuk Ching smugglers prevented transport from reaching the mother ship *Venture*.

Jack took the file, turned his back to the squad room, and headed out toward East Broadway. On the street he moved past pairs of shifty eyes, came up behind groups of Chinese men huddled outside the Fukien Employment Agency storefronts, crowded around payphones, beneath the rumble of subway trains descending along the Manhattan Bridge. The men spoke Fukienese in gruff tones, their phrases weaving, punctuated, like a cross between Vietnamese and Hakkanese. They commandeered the phones to call internationally with stolen calling cards and numbers. But Jack knew better, knew you couldn't rely on a payphone in New York City if your life depended on it. He felt the hard edge of his own cell phone in his pocket, then he was at Division Street, moving away from the crowds massing in the noonday. New immigrants, out from rent-a-bed apartments and basement subcellars.

He crossed Division to Market Street, past the Service Center, saw loitering zombies waiting to cop their methadone fixes, trade WIC coupons, food stamps, prescriptions, and then infest Chinatown seeking opportunities to steal, maybe rape. *Junkie time*, Jack called it, when parents were out at work, children at school, old folks in the park or buying the evening's groceries. Any advantage. An open window, an unguarded hand truck, a car left idling, a dangling handbag, a briefcase unattended. *Looking to get paid.*

The low-life scum of New York City, thrown down here with the Chinese because no other community wanted them, and because the Chinese were too politically impotent to fight back.

He went east again on Market until he could see Chrystie Slip, closing his mind to the ugly politics of it all.

Knowledge

The AJA, pronounced Asia, was an activist organization that got its juice from young Asian lawyers doing *pro bono* time, financed by private donations and matching government grants.

They were operating out of a converted storefront down on Chrystie Slip, where the streets left Chinatown and entered Noho.

Jack drifted past the junkie parks and the auto-repair garages until he came to what was once a bodega, under a yellow sign that read ASIAN AMERICAN JUSTICE ADVOCACY.

When he entered he saw her.

Alexandra Lee-Chow. She was thirtysomething, dressed *downtown* and wore a diamond band on her wedding finger.

The receptionist stalled him at the front desk, and watching Alexandra now, across the room, Jack began to think how uneasy women with hyphenated names made him feel. *Ambitious women.* The ones who wanted the fab careers, the motherhood, the perfect marriage, strung tight and fully charged.

Lee-Chow. Taking her husband's name but refusing to give up her own, trying to impose the past upon the future. Or maybe it was a gender power thing that came with the white collar.

She reminded him of Maylee, the type she'd become.

"Alexandra Lee-Chow," she announced to him, with a look of skeptical appraisal. "How can I help you?"

"Jack Yu," he answered. "I'm following up the Golden Venture situation."

"Right, that's what you said on the phone."

Jack saw the impatience in her eyes, and he said, "Right, a murder occurred—"

"And I *told* you they're being detained in minimum-security facilities on the East coast."

On the rag, Jack was thinking, but bit down on his tongue when she said, "*Chinese* people float around on the ocean for four months, get beaten, raped, robbed, sometimes *killed,* just to come here for freedom and a better life. You got a problem with that?"

He let a second pass, leaned back, then let the polite look leave his eyes.

"Look, *Mizz Chow,*" he said, watching her eyes narrow, "there're some bad nasty guys out there. *Specialists.* Kidnap for ransom, torture, gang rape, home invasion. They pop out eyeballs with ball-peen hammers, break ribs with baseball bats. They slice off fingers and ears. *Horrible stuff.* Ugly. Chinese, *our people.* You got the picture?"

Her eyes dropped, a moment after her jaw. Quiet.

"I think some of the men from that ship are connected to a gang war that's dropping dead bodies on my desk." He spoke at the floor. "If I came at the wrong time, I apologize, but I don't have a lot of free time and obviously neither do you."

Her face softened and she took a step back.

Jack looked at her and said quietly, "Now, if we could start over on the right foot, I'll try to be brief."

"Okay," Alexandra said, taking a breath. "Go ahead, what are you looking for?"

"Men with military backgrounds, deserters from the People's Army."

"You have names, pictures?" She raised an eyebrow.

"I've got nothing but words on the wind."

She sighed. "Well, they're all in lockup, but it's minimum security so if they decide to run, I imagine they could do it."

Jack looked across her cluttered desk. "What is their status exactly?"

She sat down. "Right now they're in limbo until the court rules. Or if the President decides to alter immigration policy."

"When does this happen?" he asked, sitting down.

"Could be a week, could be a year. We've filed a class action on their behalf, seeking political asylum."

"You mean Tiananmen Square?"

"No. We're filing on grounds that they would be persecuted for resisting abortions and mandatory sterilization."

"Have you had any interviews? Are there any claims of religious or political persecution?"

"No interviews yet. They haven't given us a schedule."

Jack thought for a long moment and was aware of Alexandra watching him. Checking her wristwatch, she said, "Look, what difference does it make? Immigration's got them and it's going to be a federal problem. Let them sort it out. And no offense, but can't the precinct find better ways to utilize manpower?"

His reverie broken, Jack said, "Excuse me?"

"*Cops,*" she said with professional disdain. "You've got gambling and prostitution all over Chinatown, and you're arresting street vendors and greengrocers."

"I'm working homicides, *Mizz Chow,*" he protested, keeping the edge on his words.

"You know what I mean." She flipped open a file on her desk, pointed to cases on a legal docket.

"I've got fifty-year-old grandmothers and teenage refugees to bail out because they sold T-shirts and socks on the sidewalk. I've got a police brutality rap from a seventeen-year-old schoolgirl, and a racism beef from a college student who argued a traffic ticket and got a busted head. I've got complaints across the board telling me how screwed up the system is."

Jack stared at her, wondering if she was mad at cops, or men, or if it was just him at the wrong time of the month.

"You think you make a difference?" she asked. "Tell me, why is it that you can't walk down the street in Little Italy, there are so many sidewalk cafés, but the Chinese guy with the fruit stand or the grandmother with the tray of socks rates a hundred-dollar summons and gets hauled away in handcuffs?"

Jack didn't know the answer to that. He said softly, "Zoning or health code, probably."

"Zoning, my ass." She leveled her gaze at him. "You know and I know, the laws aren't the same for everybody."

"I'm just doing my job," he said, tired of hearing it.

"Yes," she answered with quiet triumph. "We all have to do our jobs, don't we?" She paused for effect. "So what if a refugee woman gets kidnapped and sold as a sex slave? You turn a blind eye? Or do you make a difference?"

"I'm not working Vice, and besides you don't know how the Department works."

"I know it's not working for *us*, brother."

"Don't get righteous, *sister*, it's not becoming."

"It's *becoming* a waste of time. So, like I said, Immigration's got them and they haven't been very forthcoming with us. So, Detective, it's been real, and I know you've got to get back on the job."

Jack had nothing left so he extended his card to her, asked her to call with any new developments, a professional courtesy he'd appreciate. Alexandra Lee-Chow was checking her watch and punching up the telephone as he left her office.

Bags

Tuesday late afternoon was already as black as night. He didn't have Mona scheduled for a Tuesday pickup, but outside the China Plaza, Johnny rose out of the Continental in his black leather jacket and hustled Mona into the back seat. In the dim light, beneath her makeup, he didn't notice the blush on her cheek, under her right eye.

"I got it," he said, secretly proud of himself. "I pick it up tonight."

Mona blew him a small smile, counted out the handful of crisp new hundreds, fourteen of them, crinkling each one slightly so they wouldn't stick.

Johnny watched the focused energy in her eyes.

"*Cheen say*," he had told her, fourteen hundred, the Chinese words sounding vaguely like a *thousand deaths*. Four hundred more than Anthony "Bags" Biondo had told him the piece would cost.

Tony Biondo was a street-level goodfella, a heroin dealer for the Campesi crew that still operated out of Little Italy. They were the wiseguy remnants of the big bust-up two-year war within the Scarponelli family. Johnny knew him from the Blossom Club, where Bags liked to pick up the Malaysian hostess girls, take them to the Italian side of Mulberry Street, where he enjoyed them until daylight shone on their shame.

Johnny had met him one rainy night while waiting outside the Blossom, graciously driving Bags and a hostess the six blocks across Canal. Bags gave Johnny a twenty-dollar tip. Afterwards, Johnny noticed a glassine bag of China white on the backseat. He kept it and the next time he saw Bags, returned it to him. This act of honesty impressed Bags, and he offered his help if Johnny ever needed it.

That time had come.

Mona splayed the money evenly across the backseat. She gave Johnny a look and he knew he didn't want to ask why—he simply agreed to run the *errand*, purchase the merchandise, pocketing four hundred in the exchange. Not bad for an hours' work.

But the *silencer*, that was the surprise. A *gun* with a *silencer*, she'd said, seemingly cool even though he'd felt her fear running just beneath the surface. In an odd way he was impressed that she was exerting some control over her life. His risk, getting stung by undercover dogs, became his unspoken contribution to their *hak*, illicit, relationship.

He couldn't say no, and when he scooped the money off the seat, she leaned in and kissed him on the soft part of his throat, gathered in the fleshiness with her lips, bit him. He gave her a long hard hug, then she exited the car and went back into the high-rise, never turning her head.

Johnny watched her go, striding faster than usual, into the elevator under the soft lights, the tidy compactness of her body forming a silhouette against the blank metallic enclosure. He watched until the elevator door snapped shut and swallowed her.

He felt the wheels hop off the curb as he drove into the horizon of dull streetlamps, thinking of Tony Bags.

And the gun with the silencer.

Johnny waited as Bags climbed into the black Lincoln, the side of the car kneeling under his hulky bulk. Bags patted Johnny on the shoulder with his hammy hand, said, "C'mon, let's see the dollars, *pana*." He flared up a cigarette, powered down the window.

The way Johnny unpeeled the Ben Franklins from the wad

Mona had given him impressed the wiseguy. Bags's hand came out of his black coat and showed the piece. He opened his lips enough to let out smoke, working the cigarette over to one corner of his mouth, speaking through the other side.

"It's a Titan twenny-five caliber, six shots. Same type that Long Island Lolita bitch used. Less than a pound with the silencer. And I got you an extra magazine clip." He ran a fat finger over the ivory grips, the blue-metal finish, the knurled-steel silencer.

Johnny listened from the driver's seat, not that any of it made a difference to him, as long as it worked.

"Good up to fiteen, twenny feet." Bags grinned and pointed it in Johnny's direction a second, then aimed it out the open window and pulled the trigger.

Johnny heard the compressed suppressed explosion—*poof!*— at the same time the fluorescent sign shattered, exploded, leaving jagged plastic hanging above the Jade Takeout shop.

"It's clean right now, but it's probably got bodies on it, know what I'm sayin'?"

Johnny nodded.

"I no keepy," he said in his best English.

"You *no keepee*, you got *dat* right," chortled Bags. He popped the clip and removed the bullets, handing the goods over to Johnny. He folded the cash into his pocket and said "pussy time" with a Cheshire cat grin.

"Remember," he said, climbing out of the car, "you use it, you lose it. You get caught, you don't know nothing. *Capice?*"

"*No pobbum,*" Johnny answered, slipping the piece under his seat.

"*No pobbum, man,*" he repeated, watching Bags grease down into the Blossom.

Forgiveness

Two nights went by without a word. Her cheek, which had swelled the first day, felt normal now, but the sting of it had gone far deeper than skin and muscle. On the third day Uncle Four appeared at her door, as Mona knew he would, with roses and cognac, and a diamond tennis bracelet. She allowed him a kiss on the cheek and a fleeting hug, watching him the way an alleycat watches a bulldog.

Uncle Four wasn't apologetic, instead acted as if nothing had happened.

"It was just a misunderstanding," he declared. "You know how it is with men, this business of *bei meen*, saving face."

Mona pouted when he slipped the glittering bracelet on her wrist. He declined to summon the radio car, so they hailed a yellow cab to a fancy seafood restaurant uptown, which had a view on the Hudson River nightscape. Then he took her window-shopping along Fifth Avenue, promising her the Chanel, the Gucci, the many exquisite things he would buy her.

Mona was cool and said she'd forgotten about the incident, and before midnight came she allowed him again to enter her bedroom in the darkness above Henry Street.

She lay beneath the silk sheets, quiet after he had mounted her unsuccessfully with his horny drunk erection, finally rolling his fat weight off of her. She was pretending to be asleep.

Uncle Four was at her makeup table now, drinking again and talking on the phone with the night light on. When he was drunk this way he rambled, his voice slurring, bragging about his deals. Golo, she supposed was on the other end.

Mona lay silent, motionless, listening. She heard about the

diamonds, the big deal, something about washing money and Hakka powder.

"October eleventh," she heard, the day after the Double Ten celebration. A week away. Her eyes open in the dark now, she listened.

"The lawyer's office. *Dew keuih lo mou hei,* motherfuckers. No bodyguards. Who would dare anyway? At noon."

Uncle Four was slugging down the XO. Bragging. Laughing a pig's chortle.

"The side elevator, on Hester Street. That's the trick. *Dew!* In a plastic takeout bag from Big Wong's. Ha! You come after, with them. Together, no, we call attention to ourselves."

Then he hung up the phone, grunted, staggered back toward the bed, toward Mona, lying breathless and still.

He rolled in next to her, his hands already on her body, squeezing her breasts, her nipples, his fat fingers sliding down to her soft downy triangle, poking, violating her. He rubbed his flaccid flesh against her backside, licked his tongue against her neck, the stench of liquor on his breath.

She kept from recoiling, as she always did, even as he turned her in toward him. *The diamonds,* she thought as he pushed her head lower. *The gold coins and the big cash deal.* Her head was on the quivering round of his stomach. She opened her mouth.

Then she closed her mind.

Temple

Jack swung in for a late lunch at the Chinatown Arcade, and ordered Malaysian noodles with *satay,* peanut sauce. There was a composite sketch of the Chinatown Rapist in the window, and

Jack knew it was just a matter of time before this predator of children, was caught. Trouble was, he didn't feel it was cops who were going to nail him. The tongs had their own bounty out, and they weren't forthcoming with information.

The shop had a small shrine containing a *Kwan Kung* god flanked by red Christmas bulbs, and a mirrored *bot gwa* octagram to deflect bad spirits. The shrine made him remember Pa, and he ate his noodles toward the end of his shift thinking about the Temple he was overdue to visit.

The Grace Temple of Heaven was a Buddhist order that occupied two stories above Weinstein's Wholesale Fabrics on Orchard Street among the *Yiddishe.*

The entrance was a stairway on Allen Slip, and Jack ascended past the second floor where there was a dining hall and kitchen, where the monks prepared the vegetarian *jaai,* rice and soups, that they shared with their faithful.

He entered the temple on the third floor and looked for the monks, scanning the huge space beneath a row of gleaming crystal chandeliers. The room had a twenty-foot ceiling, which was ample height for the three ten-foot gilded Buddhas that sat on the front stage. There were prayer cushions and mats and worshippers reading from books in front of the altars, where he spotted the elder sister monk.

He went over to the table and proffered a five-dollar bill.

"*Sifu,*" he said, teacher, nodding respectfully at the shaved head with dot markings. She accepted the offering and he signed in. Behind her there was another room, which contained a wall of matchbook-size photographs attached to plastic tags with Chinese names. There was an altar there, and the flanking walls featured four-foot-tall Buddhas under glass-enclosed intricately carved pagodas.

There were smaller multi-faced and multi-armed Buddhas in gold and red, and a scattering of *kuan yin*, goddesses of mercy.

He stepped up to the altar, which was adorned with oranges and peaches, vases of gladioli, carnations, and mums. He took three sticks of incense, lit them and placed them in the lilypads of lit candles floating in a large glass urn of oil, an eternal flame.

The yellow plastic tag with Ma and Pa's names and photos was on the upper left of the wall, fitted in with a hundred others, closer to the heavenly clouds painted on the ceiling.

The humming sound he had heard upon entering the temple turned out to be the chanting of the monks, *namor namor namor*, so smooth it sounded like one word, an unending *om.*

He bowed three times, planted the other sticks of incense on the altar and stared at his parents yellow tag. *Ommmmm,* and he could feel the spirits of Ma and Pa flowing through him.

Darkness

Mona turned off the lights. The place was less ugly then. She undressed herself in the dark of Johnny's flat, then scented herself with a spray mist, sat down at the edge of his bed and waited.

Johnny stepped out of the shower, saw the blackness beyond the slit of the open door and instinctively hit the wall switch. His eyes adjusted, then he saw her clearly, seated perfectly still in the small square of moonlight that fell through the window. The only movement came from her fingers working over something hidden in her hand. He threw on a towel, watching her all the while. He heard a small humming sound coming from her as she began rocking slowly back and forth on his bed.

Water over Heaven. Auspicious sign.

Water over Heaven. Cross the river, move forward.

Buddhist, Johnny thought at first, then realized it was *Taoist* invocation.

When she saw him the spell broke.

The towel dropped as he approached her, the two of them falling together, onto the bed. She, warm and soft, and he, cold from the shower rinse, hard with desire. Yin crashing into Yang.

He turned on a small light, showing her the pistol as she pressed her softness against him. She peered along the barrel and silencer, squinted and imagined the target in her sights. She took a breath and squeezed the trigger, heard the hammer snapping down on the unloaded pistol.

"Don't worry," Johnny said. "You won't be shooting far and there's no kick."

Mona watched as Johnny chambered a round for her, flicking on the safety, then ejected the round, explaining the slide action to her.

"All you need to do is squeeze," he said. He passed the bed-sheet over the Titan in a quick wipe, cursory but careful enough to remove his prints.

Mona turned off the light on the night table, leaving the bedroom illuminated only by moonlight. She climbed on top of him and worked her body until he was hard again, inside her. Almost a half hour passed before she rolled off him.

"Will you help me load those extra bullets, my love," her lips demanded just before sliding over the head of his hardness.

In the dim light he groped for and found the extra six-shot magazine, never taking his eyes off her head, then felt again for the small box of bullets, spilling them across the night table. He was in ecstasy, his mind drifting, with clammy hands slipping the little bullets into the magazine.

Her head was bobbing, eyes open, watching him, her tongue twisting inside her mouth. He tossed the loaded clip onto the night table as her lips tightened on him, her fingernails fluttering, closing on his testes. He was ready to explode, to blast himself away from Chinatown, to a sunny place far from the reaches of the mean and unforgiving city.

Double Ten

The Kuomintang banner of the Republic of China was a twelve-pointed white sun on a dark-blue rectangle, cornered on a field of blood red. It was raised on every lamppost in Chinatown and flew along with plastic American flags over all the wide two-way avenues.

October 10th, celebrated as Double Ten, was a political holiday, the Eighty-third Anniversary of the founding of the Chinese Republic, a break away from civil war and the clutches of warlord feudalism.

Uncle Four wore his best gray suit, with a small red carnation in the lapel, beneath a red, white and blue Kuomintang flag pin.

He stood on the corner of Mott and Bayard, felt the faint sun on his face and knew exactly how it was going to happen. He'd seen it every year the last thirty years. The faces changed but the routine was the same.

He let his eyes roam over the program for the celebration. There was the Chinese Calligraphy Exhibition that the Lin Sings offered annually. Once a year the Nationalists cranked up their loudspeakers and blasted the streets with martial music, marching fanfare. In the auditorium of the Community Center there was Cantonese Opera and a Chinese Music Recital, followed by a reception—by invitation only—restricted to the big shots. They ran out the schoolchildren with candlelit Chinese lanterns and the floats with beauty queens in *cheong saams*.

Scheduled for Day Two was a late afternoon series of the Lion Dance, performed by six traditional kung fu academies. Afterward, the Gala Anniversary Dinner at twenty dollars a head, hosted by the Silver Palace and the Harmony Palace, the biggest Chinatown restaurants. The Nationalists ritually issued threats to the Chinese Communists and vowed to retake the mainland. One year they drove an armored half-track with .50 caliber machine guns and camouflage netting down Mott Street and chewed up the asphalt. The following weekend featured the Senior Citizens' presentation of Cantonese Opera, and the *bok lo*, northerners, offering Peking Opera out in Flushing. In Queens, the Nationalists from Taiwan, the Republic's forty-five-year seat of power, provided an even greater bang-up celebration of the day. That was to be expected, Uncle Four thought, Flushing being a KMT stronghold.

The wind gusted up and Uncle Four shielded his eyes from the dust. Double Ten drew people to Chinatown, *his* stronghold, and was good for business. The celebration allowed the Nationalists to blow off steam, to show off their *face* in the Chinatown power configuration: the alliances between Associations, the tongs, the *lan jai*, punk-thugs, street gangs, the Kuomintang Nationalists and the triad secret societies.

The sunny morning turned gray and blustery, the October wind carrying on it an edge of wet and cold that made the beauty queens wrap their slender arms about themselves, shiver, and scrunch up their made-up faces. The marching band from the Chinese School came down the street, a platoon of old veterans from the American Legion dragging along behind it.

Uncle Four folded the program and stepped out of the wind. He'd seen it all before and none of it held any surprises for him. He turned toward the Community Center, but was thinking about the stacks of hundred-dollar bills in the plastic takeout bag, and the cache of diamonds and gold in his bedroom that Golo had entrusted to him.

Run

In the haziness of his sleep he imagined the distant beeping of his pager singing in his ear, but when he stirred from his pillow, the sound was more distinct, a tapping on his door that made his eyes focus on the faint sliver of light and shadow that seeped in under the door from the stairwell.

He rolled off the bed, tiptoeing toward the door and the tiny hushed voice calling, *Jun Yee, Jun Yee!*

Johnny squinted through the peephole, saw it was Mona, and unlocked the double deadbolts. She brushed past him like a cold gust, saying in a rush, "You must run, the old bastard put a contract out on you." She looked desperate.

Was he dreaming? *What?* and *How?* were all he could manage against the force of her outpouring.

"There are *loong jaai*, Dragons, searching for you. Your face cannot be seen on the streets." Her body quaked in the darkness.

"He found out about us. I don't know how. I have left the apartment. I am going to *Lor Saang*, Los Angeles." Breathless, talking to him in the night shadows, her words jumped out in a steely, angry chopping rhythm.

"I *need* you. I want you to meet me there." A heartbeat passed. "Take the bus." She gave him a ticket folder, red, from Jade Tours.

He felt his heart hammering, a dryness blotting up in his throat, anguish and dread sweeping over him.

"It's all there," she said, her voice expectant.

He saw the Greyhound bus ticket, the Holiday Inn reservation, and swiveled his eyes back to her.

"I will call you in three days," she said, the moonlight flashing in her eyes. There was silence around them, his bloodshot eyes burning questions into hers.

"What's going to happen?" he finally asked, swallowing his fear.

"Don't worry. I have some money. We'll be partners." Then she turned to go and he grabbed her by the elbow. She jerked it back, tears welling up in her eyes.

"I'm going!" she cried out. "He's not going to hurt me any-more." She stepped toward him before he could wrap her closer and pounded her fists against his chest, angrily sobbing, sud-denly pushing away. "Hurry! They're after you!"

He watched her slip out the door, stunned, listening to her heels clatter down the rickety stairs. He went to the window and folded back the blinds. Saw nothing but night, streetlamps, and a yellow cab pulling away.

Under the cover of night, once she was beyond viewing from Johnny's window, Mona walked to the street phone, inserted a coin. She heard the metallic rattle, then a dial tone, and tapped in Johnny's pager sequence of eights. She took a breath, waited.

Johnny's beeper sounded before he finished buckling the belt on his jeans. In the dark of his apartment, the luminous display on his pager read 444-4444. Death numbers all across the digital display.

The old bastard seeking him.

Just like Mona had said.

He reached under the nightlight, pulled his cash and a Ruger Magnum from the floorboards under the sink. Stuffed fugitive items into a duffel bag.

He tucked the ticket folder into his pocket, stepped out into the yellow light of the stairway, moving down the steps and thinking, *Goodbye to Chinatown.*

Nite cruiser

Two A.M.

Homeless predators and mental-hospital fugitives stalked the carbon-monoxide-infused spread of the Port Authority Bus Terminal, watched warily by the sex hustlers, pimps, and returning New Jersey johns. Two PA cops patrolled together, tense, a nervous pair of birds.

Johnny kept the neat, flat packets of fifties inside the back game-pouch of his hunting vest, covered the vest under a loose-fitting barn jacket, dark, his entire presentation colorless. The Ruger in his waistband.

He went directly to a bank of telephone booths, which carried the stench of urine and stale ugly sex, nestled the greasy handset into the bend of his neck and punched in Gee Man's number. Held his breath for three rings, got a message machine.

"Take care of the car," he said. "Leave me a voice message if anyone asks for me." Stepping back from the stench, he hung up and went toward the brushed-aluminum Greyhound Star Cruiser idling at Departures.

On board he took a window seat across from the driver. The Cruiser held forty-five passengers and carried a ton of luggage in its belly hold.

He scanned the other passengers.

There were no other Chinese on the bus. Just as well. He didn't want company, small talk, or questions. The bus rolled out, only half full.

There was a group of students, a club maybe. *Baseball caps worn backwards. Jansport knapsacks.* An old white couple carrying cane suitcases. A woman and her daughter who looked Mexican. Most of the rest were hard-scrabble working-class by the look of their clothes: whites, Latinos, farm laborers, construction *dogs* returning westward, *ho*.

The Lincoln Tunnel snaked them through to New Jersey. A weariness settled over them inside the bus, a surrender, a resignation known by those who came hoping to conquer but ended up stealing away, back into exile in the dead night, their spirits swallowed whole by the unrelenting, unforgiving metropolis.

Johnny saw the last of New York City fading into the receding urban nightscape. The Greyhound pushed along, seeking the Interstate, where it could cruise at seventy-five.

His mind always came back to Mona, the idea that they could be partners. *What business could they possibly have in common?* Had she mentioned *other* partners? *Women like her had to know some big players.* He imagined a karaoke nightclub operation—something catering to an uptown clientele, until somewhere in the Pennsylvania night he realized Mona could never be more than a *silent* partner, and only in a legitimate business that wouldn't catch the attention of Big Uncle, or the Dragon Boys.

His mind drifted, different cities, different state lines. America from the Interstate, rolling by in the picture-window framed night of the Star Cruiser. *Somewhere they could blend in.* California Dreaming. Or far enough away no one would ever think to find them there. *Canada? Mexico? South America?*

But though he pondered through the night, he couldn't come up with *where* that might be.

Yin And Yang

Jack sat at the desk with the harsh daylight of the squad room window behind him, stared into the middle ground and thought of Ah Por's words, *small ears.* They made no sense.

A week had passed, more than two since the first rape, and in the zone there had been no new attacks. The pattern seemed broken, the beast gone. The community was beginning to drop its guard, strengthened by the allied tongs' pledge to bring an end to the nightmare. The composite sketches began to disappear from storefronts, from the hanging pagoda streetlamps.

Jack knew it was just a matter of time before he attacked again. He'd seen the sketch featured on an episode of *CrimeStoppers*, so he knew Sex Crimes was still active on the case.

There was a commotion downstairs, then one of the uniforms ran up and summoned Jack.

"We got a woman downstairs asking for you. They brought her in on a D and D. Lee, she said her name was."

Lee? wondered Jack, creaking down the stairs.

It was Alexandra, looking disheveled, having apparently shed the *Chow* in her last name. A female uniform, who had her by the elbow, said, "Disorderly, Detective. She was assaulting a man who claimed to be her husband. There was alcohol on her breath when we got there."

"The husband?" Jack asked Alexandra.

She didn't look at him.

"The man refused to press, but she wouldn't give it up," the uniform answered.

Jack took a breath, flashed the female cop a look that reached out saying, *Don't run her through the system.*

"I'll take it," Jack said. The officer released Alexandra's arm. Jack took her to the locker room, sat her down on one of the benches and leveled a tough look at her.

"You know you could get disbarred in New York for something as stupid as this?"

Alexandra broke down and explained tearfully how she had recently caught her husband cheating, and was feeling bitter and *volatile,* and how finally this morning, after she got back from taking her daughter Kimberly to Pre-K, she had tried to throw him out. They had fought, loud and ugly. She was throwing his clothes into the Tower's hallway when the cops came.

"What about the alcohol?" Jack asked.

"For courage." She sniffed into her handkerchief. "I had a couple along the way."

"At ten in the morning?"

"In my office." She blinked. "Leftovers from the Christmas party."

There was a short silence. He put a hand on her shoulder, and when she got up he told her to get herself a lawyer, *not* herself. Then he walked her out of the stationhouse and steered her in the direction of her daughter's schoolyard.

"Cool out," he said quietly. "Count your blessings. I know it sounds hokey, but it's never as dark as you think. Okay?"

"Okay," she answered, gratitude and shame in her trailing voice as she hurried down the street.

When he returned to the locker room, he noticed the handkerchief on the bench. It was Chinese silk, embroidered in red with the monogram AL. He picked it up and stuffed it into his jacket pocket, not really caring whether or not she'd return for it.

Highway

Johnny fell asleep at dawn, Ohio, Indiana, somewhere. When he awoke it was afternoon, the bus pushing on, the highway changing to a two-lane blacktop ribbon and back to the Interstate again. By sunset they rolled into St. Louis.

He ate fried eggs at the Terminal Diner, washed his stubbled face in the men's-room sink. He called Gee Man again. Still no answer.

At night he stayed awake, watching the changing of passengers on the Greyhound, saw the night lights going by at a distance from the highway. He felt safe near the driver, the Ruger nestled in his waistband holster, his cash stash flat against his back.

The air got thin and cool as the bus climbed the pitch-black night toward the mountains. *Worse came to worse, sell the Lincoln to Gee Man, make up a sweetheart lease or something. Wire the money out slow and easy.*

He bought a throwaway razor kit in Denver, shaved in the station's washroom, rinsed the dead taste from his mouth. When he called Gee Man he got the machine again.

123

Dewwww, he cursed, *fuckit,* and hung up.

Daylight came again.

He wasn't too concerned about Gee Man now. It was Los Angeles—and Mona—that was dancing in his mind.

In the desert everything became clear, the air light and transparent over white sand that shouldered up to the highway. The visibility was endless along the mysterious monochromatic landscape.

The bus rolled toward the smog-clouded city, becoming one with the tangle of freeway interchanges, slogging along on swooping ribbons of concrete.

It reminded Johnny of New York City.

Here, three thousand miles away, he gave in to the momentary belief that he was safe from Uncle Four and his mob. They had no pictures of him. *What were they going to do? Phone in a description across the country?*

Murder

Jack lay in a dead sleep until the phone jangle bolted him, jerked his groggy head off the pillow to hear Sergeant Paddy Murphy's growl.

"Detective Yu!" Paddy barked.

"Yeah, it's me, Sarge." The clock showed a fuzzy high noon.

"We had a full moon last night. Loony tunes. Captain wants ya down quick. You got a hot one on Hester, number four-four-four. You'll see the uniforms there. Hurry it up!"

Jack dropped the receiver, picked it off the floor, replaced it on its cradle. He rolled his neck and groaned, took five fast and deep *tai chi* breaths thinking, *Chinatown Chinatown Chinatown.*

He pulled on his clothes, strapped on his revolver, grabbed his knapsack and before the cold splash of water dried on his face, was out the door.

He arrived at the scene in twelve minutes, the dome on the Fury roof flashing, the siren wailing, as he sped across the Brooklyn Bridge. He arrived before the EMS crew, and the uniforms took him, jogging, up to the third floor.

He caught his breath and saw the victim on the floor, half-in half-out of the side elevator, the doors bumping up against his waist, opening and closing again.

"Shut it down," Jack said to the custodian.

"Sorry, Detective," the uniform said. "Sarge said not to touch anything till you got here."

"It's okay." Jack scanned the gathering of curious office workers. "Any statements?"

"No one saw anything, or heard anything. Typical."

"That so? *Typical?*"

The patrol officer looked away sheepishly.

"Who found him?" Jack relented.

"The watchman at the door downstairs."

"Bring him up."

Jack shot the roll of film, covering all the angles, then pocketed the plastic camera. He leaned over the short heavyset body, sidestepping the blood pooling around the man's head. There was a gold band on his wedding finger. A diamond ring on his other hand. The face was bloody, looked contorted where it had slammed into the linoleum floor. Jack put his fingers on the man's neck, felt it was still warm, but there was no pulse.

The gray Hong Kong silk suit jacket had fallen open. Jack fished out a wallet and a ring of keys. Turning his back to the elevator, he went through the wallet while pacing to the far wall. He ran his hand along the wall at eye level, then stepped back, reached lower and ran his hand along it again. He found a small hole. He took out his penknife and dug out a section of the sheetrock. The squashed slug was a small caliber. Twenty-two long, maybe a twenty-five automatic. *Handgun,* he thought, *at close range.* There were no shell casings in the elevator car.

From the wallet he pulled a driver's license, a credit card. *Wah Yee Tam, aged sixty.* Had an address at Confucius Towers. *Uncle Four,* he suddenly realized.

There was a lawyer's business card showing an address in the building. Another card for a limo service. He made a mental log of the items.

The watchman came up. He said in halting Toishanese how he came upon the victim.

"I was making the rounds. The *sing song gay,* elevator, was stuck on the third floor and I went to check. The security camera out front was working, but the tape had already run out. It's the door custodian's responsibility, but he went to get takeout."

Jack showed him the lawyer's card. The man was hesitant, looked away and said, "That's his lawyer."

"You know them?" Jack squinted at him.

"Not personally, I mean. Just see them in the building."

"A lot?"

"Regular." He glanced at his watch, stared out the window, didn't say anything more. Jack felt the aura of death and bad luck around them.

"Leave your name and number with the officer," Jack cautioned him. "And get the elevator engineer to meet me in the basement."

The medical examiner arrived and Jack left him with the EMS, and the Crime Scene Unit, then hoofed it up the stairwell to the lawyer's office on Five.

The lawyer, C.K. LOO, JD, CPA, MBA, CFP, appeared to be in shock and was little help.

"I wasn't expecting him," he said vacantly, "but it's Double-Ten time. Maybe he came to extend salutations."

"Was that his habit?"

"During holidays, yes."

"Do you know of any reason why someone would want him killed?"

"None whatsoever. Everything's aboveboard."

"Is there a will?"

"Yes."

"Who benefits?"

C.K. Loo was monotone. "His wife, his daughter."

"Do you know if he carried life insurance?"

"Yes."

Jack stepped closer. "How much?"

"Two hundred thousand."

"The beneficiary?"

"His wife."

Jack scanned the man's desk, said softly, "How do you know all this?"

"My brother sold him the policies." He rubbed his forehead, adjusted his spectacles.

"What else?"

"Nothing." Loo shook his head.

Jack handed him a business card. "Hang around. I may have more questions."

C.K. sighed, shook his head some more. "A terrible thing," he said, "to die like that."

Jack left the stunned lawyer and went back to speak with the Medical Examiner. The paramedics had the body bagged and were rolling it out to the van on a gurney.

"I'll have an answer tonight," the M.E. said, packing his tools. He left and Jack watched the custodian mopping up the blood and the bad-luck superstition.

Afterward Jack went down to the basement, had the engineer bring the elevator halfway up. Jack borrowed his flashlight, checked the sides and the bottom of the elevator pit. No shell casings. *Revolver,* he thought, *but no one heard anything. If a silencer was used, the weapon would have to have been an automatic, but he couldn't imagine a pro hitter stopping to pick up the shells. Unless it wasn't a pro. Unless the building workers did hear something but were just being Chinese, afraid to get involved with the law.* Considering the contradictions, he returned to the lobby, felt the dead man's keys jangling in his jacket pocket. Six brass-colored keys on the ring. He saw that three keys had the word *Kong* stamped on them. The name of the locksmith, probably. The other three keys were newer, stamped *Klein Hdw,* a hardware-store set. He wondered what doors they would lead him to, and dropped them back into his pocket.

"*Setup,*" he said to himself, *revenge or money,* and headed for the Thirty Minute Photo Shop.

Rage

Golo crossed Hester Street, avoiding the uniform cops who were cordoning off the building's entrance with yellow crime-scene tape. The Hakkas followed a safe distance behind him, disappearing into the backstreets with their China White Number Four.

Back in his apartment, Golo took the Tokarev out from under his bed, loading it with an urgency that made his hand tremble when he inserted the clip. A scattering of images crossed his mind as he slid the pistol into the holster under his arm. *Fifty thousand in Pandas and diamonds.* He paced the apartment chainsmoking cigarettes, figuring it out. *Mona, the whore. Had to be her.* The old man must have blabbed about it. *Forget it,* bak gee seen—*paper fan rank—was out of the question now. Lucky if they didn't kill him even if everything was recovered. The bitch,* he thought, as he ran out of the apartment, *was going to pay big when he caught up with her.*

He waited on the street outside the China Plaza, nodded toward a sedan full of Dragons, before he fell in behind the Chinese mailman and entered the building.

Golo took the elevator to Mona's condo and crowbarred the lock, buckling the door frame as he forced it. He slipped out the nine-millimeter, stepped inside the large room. *Empty.* As he had feared, he was too late. The bed was made, nothing under it. He pushed back the accordion doors of the closet, saw belts, scarves, designer jackets and dresses with fancy labels. On the floor were more than a dozen shoeboxes, and a set of matching leather bags in different sizes. *She left in a hurry.* He holstered the gun, went through the lingerie and linens in the drawers. In the kitchenette cupboard, spices, chrysanthemum tea bags, plastic dishes, a set of tableware, were stacked neatly in place. A scattered mound of mahjong blocks was on the counter. The refrigerator was empty.

He found toothpaste, a bottle of astringent, in the bathroom.

Golo tossed the furniture quickly, found nothing. He went back down to the street, posted a Dragon at the entrance and sent one up to the apartment. He instructed the *dailo,* "Find me a black radio car with triple-eight—*bot bot bot*—license plates. It waits at a cab stand in front of Confucius Towers sometimes.

Check out the garages along the backstreets. Bring in the driver."
Golo's hard eyes narrowed. "For questioning."

Actress

Tam *tai* was the grieving widow draped in black, sobbing, hanky dabbing at her eyes, streaks of liner running. She was supported on the couch by Mak *mui* and Loo *je*. Jack smelled the heavy incense and saw the *bot kwas* facing out every window.

The only jewelry Tam *tai* wore was dark brown jade bracelets.

She spoke haltingly, with a slight Taiwanese accent. "He was a good man, I don't know who would want to kill him. The On Yees were his rivals, but everyone agrees there was peace this year."

Jack took a breath through his nose.

"Forgive me for mentioning, but there's the matter of the life insurance."

Tam *tai* didn't flinch, her gaze moving around the expanse of the living room.

"Take a look, detective," she said solemnly. "Take a good look around you." She paused for effect. "Do I look like a woman who needs money?"

Loo *je* and Mak *mui* flashed indignant glances at him. Jack nodded respectfully as she smiled bravely.

"He had stomach problems the last two years. We were fortunate to get extra term life insurance." She sniffed, accepted tissues from Loo *je*.

"There was a whole life policy he had for forty years and he felt it wasn't enough. He had a daughter also, you must know."

Jack knew, but it wasn't any help.

"Where is she?" he asked.

"She's attending college in *Saam Fansi*, at USF, but she's returning tonight."

Easy enough, he thought, *to check her class schedule and call her professors, to verify her alibi.*

"Where was he yesterday?"

"It was Double Ten. He had affairs to attend, with the Association: dinner, reception. He wasn't home until after ten."

"Could you be more precise?"

"I was in bed, but I heard him lock the door."

"When did you actually see him last?"

"We had breakfast this morning. He went out about eleven."

"Did he say he was meeting someone?"

"No, he never discussed his private business with me." She started sobbing again.

He produced the ring of keys. "These were in his pocket. Are they the keys to this apartment?"

She took a closer look.

"I'm not sure," she said. "My set is on the tray, on the stand by the door."

He went over and sized them up. Her set of three, in a leather case, was also stamped *Kong*, and was a perfect match. He came back to her.

"These other three," he asked, "are they for here?"

"No." Her breath was short, quick. "Perhaps the Association."

"*Ah sir*," Loo *je* said sternly, "she must rest now. There are long hours ahead, and she needs to be strong."

Mak *mui* stood up, supporting the unsteady widow.

Jack again offered his condolences, gave Tam *tai* his police card and left them. When the door closed behind him he heard the sudden burst of wailing within, the *gwa foo*, widow, dowager, anguishing for her *lo gung*, husband.

Old Men

Jack turned the corner onto Pell, going in the direction of the Hip Ching clubhouse. Long ago, the storefront clubhouse was where the Hip Chings had kept the cleavers, the long knives, axes and hammers, an occasional pistol. It was from there that they would strike out, across Doyer, the Bloody Angle, *bow how doy*—hatchet men—searching for On Yee fighters on the other side of Mott.

Now, the older members gathered here to meet, play mahjong, gossip, make assorted deals with the Chings' Credit Union. They no longer kept weapons there. The gang boys were packing them now, strapped on, outside on the streets.

Jack stepped into the storefront, into the dimly lit fluorescent space with wooden chairs lining the green walls. A partition closed off the back of the place. The clubhouse was empty, not even the old man sweeper who usually hung around chain smoking cigarettes, waiting for tips, was there. They must have seen the *chaai lo*—cop—coming, Jack figured, must have exited the back door, to meet again at the Association, or in one of the coffee shops they operated.

Their little game didn't faze Jack. He was sure he'd find the old men soon enough. They were, after all, obligated to stick around for the funeral. He began to wonder if the murder was an On Yee double cross, and spent an hour working the dingy little coffee shops, leaving behind his bilingual calling card, seeking clues he knew would turn up in more than one language.

The entrance to the Hip Ching Benevolent Association was a gold-colored tile pagoda on top of cast bronze doors that opened to a red stairway leading up. Inside, the furniture was all black Taiwanese mahogany with crimson cushions flattened by the weight of old men.

The Hip Ching big shots said nothing of value to Jack, feigned ignorance because *face* overwhelmed everything else. *How could they mention the mistress and dishonor their leader and his family in this cycle of grieving?*

"Could it have been a grudge from the old days?" Jack asked.

"Everyone from the old days is dead. He was the last."

Jack showed them the keys.

"Except for the front, downstairs, our doors have no locks," one of the elders said. "There is a safe, but it has a combination lock. At any rate, Uncle wasn't involved in everyday affairs, only special events."

The old men could have saved Jack some time by continuing to dummy up. Instead, they offered up the Fuk Chou: Fukienese, newcomers, outsiders, troublemakers, claiming *they* were robbing Association member businesses at the outer edge of Chinatown. Uncle Four had issued warnings to them but had received only mocking derision in return. *Ho daai dom,* ballsy, those Fuk Ching *kai dais,* shitheads.

Jack had the uneasy feeling that he was being manipulated, but he thanked the old men, playing them the way they played him, the *chaai lo*—cop. They each shook his hand on the way out. Patted him on the back. Wished him good fortune. Outside the double doors, on the street, Jack smelled kitchen aromas venting into the sunset air, the restaurants firing up their woks for the dinner crush. He felt a gnawing hunger, but forced himself to isolate probable motives: money, or revenge. Or both. Forty-eight hours had passed, the trail was getting cold. He had the feeling that the killer had already bounced, and the only keys around weren't opening up any new doors.

Fuks

Carved with broad strokes into the black wooden board and gilded over with gold leaf, the Chinese characters announced Fuk Chou Village Benevolent Association. Beneath the sign the double door opened into a small office with a large window, looking out over East Broadway where it intersected with Pike below, Essex at the far corner.

The Chinese man behind the metal desk evaded Jack's questions, occasionally glancing at the video security monitor that focused on the door and the street below. The man was about sixty, balding, with an officious and gracious manner that began to sour the more Jack talked.

"We know," Jack said, "you run a gambling operation downstairs, in the back."

"Then you know," the man answered, "we paid this month already. What did you think, because you're Chinese you get an extra share?"

"Look, Uncle, a bigshot was murdered. Some voices say the Fuk Ching are responsible."

"You *chaai lo* are all the same, running dogs trying to squeeze more juice from hard-working brothers."

The words grated on Jack, made him hot under the collar. "I can subpoena your members, your records," he threatened.

The man grinned. "There is nothing to see, no one to speak to. We have nothing to hide."

Jack kept his poker face on.

"I can shut down the Twenty-Eight," he said.

The man whitened, glared at him.

"I see now, the Ghost Legion pays your salary."

Jack leaned in, said in a hard whisper, "Be careful, old man, your words may hang you one day."

The man looked out the window.

"First you send your punks to rob us, then comes the cop to finish it."

Jack's eyes widened. "There was no robbery report."

"Report what? To bring more dogs running?"

Jack's look devoured the man, but he said nothing. There was a long silence between them, then Jack pushed out of his chair and brushed back the side of his jacket, hand on his hip, exposing the Colt in the holster there.

A look of fear crossed the man's face.

Jack grinned, wagged a finger at him, said, "You have a sharp tongue for an old man. Careful you don't cut yourself." He turned and left the office, quick-stepped down the stairs.

If it wasn't a Fuk Ching execution, he was thinking, then it had to involve a double cross.

Clarity

Jack sank into his chair in the squad room, sliding the backs of his fingers across the hard stubble of his chin while contemplating the photographs from the Thirty Minute Photo. He'd started a new file under the heading WAH YEE TAM/Uncle Four, and was attaching the pictures when the phone rang.

"Fifth Squad," he answered. "Detective Yu."

It was the Medical Examiner.

"Small caliber," the M.E. said, "probably a twenty-five. From one to two feet, we got powder marks. The slug entered left back of the head, went through bones in the cranium. There's a piece in the frontal lobe just inside the forehead. That's the one that killed him. There's another entry wound further toward the center of the head that exited the top of the skull. Shot as he was falling forward."

There was a pause before he continued.

"The killer's probably right-handed, short, and the victim was dead before he hit the ground. I call it about eleven fifty-five a.m."

Not your average hitman's caliber of choice, thought Jack. Three-eighty, nine-millimeter, he could see. The twenty-two, the twenty-five, was a lady's round, made for those little pistols that looked like cigarette lighters, the ones with plastic pearl handles, toylike, plated gold or chrome.

The M.E. hung up and Jack made the entries in the file, thinking, *A big shot got whacked just before noon on a working holiday, a Saturday in Chinatown. Offices in the building open but nobody heard anything. Were they just being Chinese? Or did the shooter have a silencer? Empty elevator. No witnesses.*

The setup was too good, Jack decided. Someone had gotten real close, someone the victim knew.

Payback

The item appeared in the late edition of the *Daily News*, a two-inch column in the Metro Section, sandwiched between a photo of an auto accident and a piece on condoms in schools. The headline ran "Man Shot in Chinatown" under which it read:

A man believed to be the undersecretary of the Hip Ching Benevolent and Labor Association, a Chinatown tong, was fatally shot near his lawyer's office yesterday, police said. Wah Yee Tam, 60, was found shot in the head execution style en route to his lawyer's office at 444 Hester Street at about noon. Police have no suspects and could not comment on motive, but they voiced the fear that the shooting signals a resumption of local gang warfare. Anyone with information is urged to call (212) 334-0711. All calls will be kept confidential.

In The Wind

The Yellow Cab had jerked to a stop.

Mona kicked out of the side door onto the curb, hurried toward the rush of commuters. She was a shapeless form, her head wrapped by the Hermès scarf, eyes hidden behind the Vuarnets, a black garment bag slung over her shoulder, as she stepped onto the escalator, plunging her down into the sea of heads. Inside, Penn Station was a blur of video digital displays, flashing yellow lights, red uniforms hunkered down in glass bunkers designated TICKETS, RESERVATIONS, DEPARTURES.

She left the baggy brown Chinese jacket she'd worn in the ladies' room, emerged in a black leather blazer, the scarf tied around her neck. All in black now.

The rental locker opened with a snap of the key, and she

pulled out a hard-molded Samsonite Rollmaster, black with steel hardware, pulling it behind her as she drifted into the surging merging crowds, moved along by the blaring loudspeakers. She checked her watch as she went, weaving through the other travelers onto the platform, beneath the cool fluorescent lights, past the silvery metallic trains, past the throbbing engines.

Her private accommodations were on a sleek SuperLiner, the Broadway Limited, in a deluxe bedroom sleeper compartment that had its own shower and toilet, and an extra bed folded into the wall.

The trainman took her ticket, punched it, noticed her cherry lipstick and fingernails. He smiled, nodded, went his way down the platform. She stepped up into the Slumber Coach room, hung the garment bag and took the Vuarnets off. Closing her eyes a moment, she took a deep breath. Then again.

She locked the door, sat on the fold-down bed and removed a bottle of XO from the Rollmaster. She took a swallow to calm herself, lit up a Slims, opened the window.

The Broadway Limited pulled out of Penn Station and went west under the Hudson, emerging in the New Jersey Palisades. The cigarette burned down as she watched the New York City skyline blend into the overcast afternoon, into the rush of mountain scenery. She leaned back, blew smoke, and contemplated what she had done.

Killshot

The old bastard never recognized her. She'd worn a shoulder-length shag-cut wig, black with chestnut highlights, and streaked with amber. A deep red on her lips. With the French sunglasses that made her appear twentysomething, she'd looked like someone else entirely. *He never saw it coming.* A black garment bag draped horizontally along her left arm, the little gun folded inside the bag's zip-pocket. *No one else around.*

There was a scarf wrapped inside her black leather blazer, all of it covered by an oversized student jacket that looked like cheap Chinese polyester. *He was there, with the plastic bag, momentarily surprised to see her, a siu jeer, a young street girl.* The elevator door opened, they stepped in. He smiled, looked away. She pressed three, stepped back as the doors closed. Behind him now, she raised the garment bag. *There was no turning back. Time to say goodbye.* The doors opened and she squeezed the trigger once, twice, into the back of his head, the little shells ejecting inside the garment bag. She grabbed the plastic takeout sack as he fell forward, stepped over his body, heard a gurgling noise, and hurried down the back stairwell.

Out onto the street. A block away, she shed the wig, slipped the scarf up over her head like a cowl, going quickly down to where Center Street became Lafayette and the traffic ran north.

She hid behind the French sunglasses and waved her arm at the oncoming traffic.

The streets flashed past through the cab window. She shifted the gun back into the fold of the zip-pocket, dared enough to glimpse gold coins and cash inside the takeout bag, and knew there had to be diamonds. Time rushed by under the traffic lights, and she started up a cigarette, imagining the urgent wail of police sirens, ambulances. The cab turned west, rolled through a green light and continued north on Eight Avenue.

She smoked the cigarette down to the filter, snuffed it in the side ashtray. Wiped her lipstick, checked her watch. Twelve-fifteen. *Twenty-eighth Street, Thirtieth.* She got a ten ready, didn't want to look back when she left the cab. The streets ran by until Penn Plaza loomed up.

Wisdom

Jack had dinner alone, a plate of onion-smothered grilled steak at the back table of the Golden Star. Chased it with a beer, waited while surfing TV news channels. *President Clinton setting up Japan for the biggest bash of all. North Korea, nuclear rogue of Asia. China, remember Tiananmen Square, the Most Favored Nation.*

When Alexandra arrived they took a back booth and sat opposite each other in the shadowy blue light. He ordered another beer and she started with a Kamikaze.

"Thanks for coming," he said.

The mood was conciliatory. Jack lit both their cigarettes as she said, "You did me a favor. I owe you."

"You don't owe me anything," he replied. "I know you're trying to do something positive, trying to make a difference. I didn't want to see that going down the drain."

Alexandra blew smoke sideways, assessed him with her eyes. "Well," she began, "you'll be happy to know, Immigration's got them."

"*Them?*" he said, leaning in across the table.

"*Sixteen* of them actually. With military tattoos. National Security turned two of them and the others fell into place. They're wanted by the Chinese military police, and Federal's going to turn them over."

"Flight deportation?"

"Full Air Force escort." She cut a small smile as the drinks arrived.

"Banzai." He grinned, clinking his beer against her Kamikaze, both of them gulping the drinks.

"Thanks," he said quietly. "Must be a little disappointing to you, since you see them as victims, people you feel a calling to defend and protect."

Alexandra swirled the ice in her glass.

"You mean as compared to how you see them, as *perps*, Chinese who prey on other Chinese? And since your calling obligates you to take them off the streets?"

"We don't see them the same way," Jack agreed, "but that doesn't make either of us wrong."

Alex nodded, "But sometimes it puts us on different sides."

Jack looked away. "We can still be friends."

"Friends, sure," she answered.

They shook hands, his firm grip covering the soft squeeze of her hand. There was a momentary twinkle in her eyes before she looked away.

"There's some split public opinion about sending the others back," she said. "If we don't take the Cubans, or the Haitians, we can't take the Chinese."

Jack nodded, let her run on.

"But Clinton's got to take a stand on Human Rights some-where, especially after Tiananmen Square. Send a message to Comrade Deng."

Jack grinned.

"It's a tough call," she continued. "There's a pro-life movement stirring in Congress. The Right wants to keep them, use them as a symbol. Could be a long wait. But my guess is they'll stay."

There was a pause. They exhaled smoke toward each other, and she drained her drink. Ordered another. Even in the dim light he could see the color coming hard into her face. He didn't want to ask about the husband, the situation, didn't want to open up that conversation.

He watched her work the second Kamikaze, giving him a glance that was slowly coming unfocused.

She lit another cigarette, softened her tone. "Look, I know you're busy," she said. "This godfather from Pell Street who got killed, it's all over the news."

"Yeah, got us all running around in circles."

"Must be difficult for you."

"You know how Chinatown works."

"Not that, I mean getting justice for a victim you know is organized crime."

"I'd rather leave that judgment to a jury. Someone kills someone, they got to pay. That's the law."

"The law, yeah, I know something about that. So how's the investigation going?"

"People are watching their tongues. Except for you and some fifty-year-old police records, I can't find a bad word anywhere."

"It's too soon. People are eulogizing him, they're showing respect. Maybe after the funeral."

Jack's winced. "By then, my killer's out of the country."

She gave him a curious look, excused herself to the ladies' room. He paid the bill before she returned.

"Thanks for the drinks," she said on the way out. "I had you wrong. You're a decent guy and you know the score."

"Fair enough," Jack smiled. "Thanks for your help."

She flagged a cab, stepped off the curb, puzzled a moment before reaching into her handbag, producing a business card. *Luen Hop Kwok*, the *United National*, was embossed across the card. At the bottom, Vincent Chin, *reporter.*

"Call him," she said. Then she ran her fingers sweetly across his cheek before kissing him, got into the cab, slammed the door.

Jack stood watching the rear window rolling away, Alexandra's face a sad smile under the lamp light. He moved toward the backstreets, resigning himself to the Federal guys coming in and sucking up the whole mess. He couldn't complain. He had a bigger headache throbbing right behind his eyes.

News

The copy from the *Daily News* was translated into the Chinese language dailies, which also added sidebars about the crowning achievements in the *revered leader's* life: he raised money for the Chinatown Daycare Center, operated a fund for widows and orphans, organized food and clothing donations to the needy, the elderly, the infirm. He was a Chinese saint.

The Hip Chings posted a fifty-thousand-dollar reward for information.

Jack tossed through the newspapers, knew he had to go beyond the machinations of the press, find what wasn't being written, neighborhood gossip and speculation not fit for print. He wanted unsubstantiated chatter from old women, the words of whores, of shiftless men in smoky coffee shops. The backstreets led him toward White Street, where he flipped the business card, and called Vincent Chin.

Chinatown's oldest newspaper, the *United National,* was located on White Street, nestled down behind the Tombs Detention Facility and the Federal buildings across from the Men's Mission.

The paper operated out of a renovated storefront in a building that was once a warehouse, a five-story brickfaced structure with ornate iron columns framing fire-escapes that jagged across the front exposure.

The *National* had a staff of twenty that included pressmen, reporters, editors, photographers, and managers. Compared to the other major Chinese dailies, it couldn't claim the highest circulation, or the lowest newsstand price. In fact, the *National* was the only paper without a color section, the only Chinese newspaper that still typeset by hand the thousand Chinese characters it needed to go to print. They had special typewriters for the different fonts, other machines for headlines and captions.

The *United National* sold for forty cents a copy and appeared on the newsstands every day but Sunday.

The *National* was Chinatown's hometown paper.

It had been Pa's favorite, his *only* newspaper.

Clue

Vincent Chin said in bilingual-accented English, "What we're not writing is that Big Uncle had a mistress, that the killing was a Hakka drug deal that got twisted somehow. It's hearsay. We can't prove it, we can't print it."

Jack kept fishing. "Other enemies? A double cross?"

"Some people suspect the Ghosts, others say the Dragons, or the Fuk Ching. It's Chinatown fantasy as far as I'm concerned."

"What about the mistress?"

"It's gossip. Someone spotted her in a gambling house. But no one's come forward with a picture, an address, or a body."

"If you had a mistress, wouldn't you keep it hushed up?"

"Yes, but it's Chinatown. You can't shut down loose talk. That's all it is."

"How'd you hear?"

"People call up. You can't imagine the calls we got."

"That's why I'm here." Jack checked his watch, almost nine p.m. "Was it a man who called, or a woman?"

"A man," Vincent said. "Does it matter?"

"I don't know." Jack left his cop card on the typewriter. "But if there's anything else you can think of . . ."

"I'll call you, or Alex."

"Perfect. Thanks for your time," Jack said, and shook Chin's hand.

Outside, Jack took a deep swallow of the cool night air and trailed the backstreets of Chinatown, letting murder and motive tumble around in his head. When no answers fell out, he took a long look at the basements running down Mott Street under colored neon lights, and remembered Tat "Lucky" Louie.

He nursed two cups of coffee at the Me Lee Snack shop, eavesdropping on Hip Ching gossip: old men's chatter about a fight at a karaoke club. *Hong Kong bitch* was the last phrase he picked out of the thick Toishan accents.

Then he returned to Pa's apartment and ate monk's vegetarian *jaai,* studied the pictures of the dead man, and waited for midnight to drop.

Number Nine Hole

The room was a hazy brightly lit basement, thick with the smell of whiskey, coffee, and cigarettes. They were two-fifty, say three-hundred people crammed together, Chinese men shoulder-to-shoulder, three deep at the gaming tables. Dragon Ladies serving XO and coffee to the high rollers.

Jack stepped into this eclectic mix of waiters, businessmen, hoodlums, cowboys, and street-gang kids. He saw how the younger men seemed to group together, how the Ghostboys had a certain swagger here, the throng parting for their every move from table to table. No doubt who this place answered to. The anxious crowd played *mahjong, fan tan, paigow*, thirteen-card poker, betting on fighting fish every half hour. Eight tables were working hard, especially at consuming the whiskey they were spreading around. Jack played the tables along the fringe, leading to the far back of the long room. There was a door there. The little white fan-tan buttons weren't turning up right; it cost Jack a ten-spot to watch that door. They all shifted, now betting at the thirteen-card table, almost at the far end. Another ten-spot rode his hand against the House. He saw some of the young guns exit through the doorway which led to a back room and a connecting courtyard. Jack's cards won heads and tails, suddenly upping him twenty bucks. He picked up his money and moved smoothly toward the doorway.

A procession of street kids cut him off. He was letting them drift by when he felt the bump, the heft, of gun-barrel metal jammed into his side, just below the ribs. "Move," the voice said. Before he could turn he was swept up by a crew of Ghost Legion darkshirts, pushed into the back room, where another gun pressed into his temple. He was turned around, slowly, arms stretched sidewise. He felt hands yank the Colt Special from his waist, brought his eyes to bear on a familiar face, fuller now and jowly, with a thickset body, leaning to one side. Around him hate was beaming from Ghost faces, just itching for trouble.

Jack felt the heavy metal slide away from his temple, saw the man step back, a disgusted look on his face. The man reached across Jack's neck and lifted the chain with the detective's badge dangling from it.

"Tat Louie," Jack said.

Lucky let the chain run across his fingers before he balled up his fist and yanked the badge from Jack's neck.

"You gotta lotta balls coming to squeeze me," he said. "That badge ain't shit down here."

"If I wanted to squeeze you I wouldn't have come alone."

"Hey, I'm pissing, I'm so scared," Lucky hissed. "What the fuck you want coming down here?"

"I need help, Tat."

"You need help, call nine-one-one," he cracked. The Ghosts howled.

"That's funny, Tat. Just like it's funny how somebody whacked Uncle Four and nobody knows nothing."

Lucky almost smiled. "Don't worry about it, Jacky boy; you know, it's Chinatown."

Jack straightened. "I know eight months ago you made peace with the Black Dragons. Uncle Four set it up and put his name on it."

The Ghosts spread back, giving them some room.

"Yeah, so you know it wasn't us," Lucky said, holstering the heavy Python revolver.

"Maybe there was a double cross." Jack grinned.

"Maybe you should go fuck yourself," Lucky said, lighting up a cigarette. He blew smoke into Jack's face.

"It wasn't random, wasn't a robbery. More like a pro job," Jack said through the haze. "Was it the White Tigers? Born to Kill, the Fuk Ching?" Jack hesitated.

"Yeah, it was alla them, especially them little Fuk Chow pricks."

147

"Come on, Tat, let's deal. I know you got problems."

"Do I look worried?" He blew more smoke at Jack.

"You should be. The Fuks and the Namese boys been chopping you up."

Lucky chortled, took a drag on the cigarette. "You crack me up," he said, the others sneering behind him.

"You gave up Market Street," Jack pressed.

"What the fuck you smoking, man?"

"Come on, Tat, let's deal."

"Deal? You got nothing I want."

"They say he had a girlfriend, brought her gambling."

"You're wasting my time, Jacky boy."

"Now she's disappeared too."

"Don't know nothing about it."

"Hong Kong type. A karaoke singer?"

"Can't help you, man."

Jack took a breath, hadn't expected to last this long and knew he was on a roll.

"Yeah," he said, "but I can help you. I can make it tough for the Fuk Ching. I can have their cars towed."

Lucky wasn't impressed, blew smoke from his nose.

"I can put heat on their gambling joints," Jack pushed on. "I can roust the Namese boys, shake them up a little."

Lucky seemed vaguely interested now. "Keep talking," he said.

"I need a face, a name." Jack was fishing deeper water now. "I can access the department's computers, find out where all your enemies are."

"And you don't care one bit if we whack them all," Lucky spit out contemptuously.

"I do not give a fuck," Jack said. "I wish you all would whack each other out the same day. Make my job a lot easier."

"Bring me some information," Lucky said, snuffing the cigarette.

"I need a face, a name."

"You're chasing shadows, man. It's smoke."

"So we dealing or what?"

Lucky was intrigued now, though he couldn't show it in front of the Ghosts. He said, "Give me a sign, Jacky. I'll be listening."

The darkshirts whisked Jack through the courtyard, through a hallway leading to a side street. Lucky held up Jack's chain, let the badge dangle before he tucked it into Jack's pocket.

"You got some fuckin' balls coming down here, boy," he said, suddenly snapping an uppercut into Jack's gut, a sucker punch driving Jack to his knees. As the Ghosts moved off laughing, Jack gasped for air and heard Lucky grinning words through his teeth.

"That's for old times," he snapped.

Busted

When dawn faded in, an FBI/DEA task force took down the Fuk Chou Association leadership, arresting nineteen illegals in connection with the murders in Teaneck and the grounding of the Golden Venture.

Public Morals Division came and shut down the Twenty-Eight after complaints surfaced from gamblers who'd been robbed there.

At noon, Jack watched as the Department of Transportation brownshirts hitched up a line of parked cars, saw the scowls on young Fuk Ching faces as municipal tow trucks hauled away their Firebirds/Trans Ams/Camaros. The trucks lurched off Lafayette, then headed west toward the piers as Jack turned in the direction of Mott Street.

Things were getting stirred up on East Broadway, and Jack was happy to take credit for it.

Send a message to Lucky, he was thinking.

Ghost Brother

The gray nimbostratus sky of October floated in from the Atlantic, dropped over Chinatown in an uncertain change of seasons, from a summer that had been boiling hot to a lifeless autumn that muted the changing of colors.

Gray clouds drifted past the red pagoda motif of the On Yee building, down the ceramic tilework, the wind whipping up the Association's red, white, and black banner, the cloth cut jagged along its perimeter so that it appeared to be a dragon's tail.

Lucky stood beneath the banner, plugged into a Walkman, and lit up. K-Rock on the airwaves.

From the rooftop he could see all of Chinatown, from the river to the east, and west as far as the unending line of tractor trailers dodging into the Holland Tunnel.

He looked north, seeing past Little Italy as far as Soho. South, he saw the Jersey shoreline where it crept behind the torch of Liberty, just barely visible above the city skyline.

He could see across the Manhattan Bridge running east-west to Brooklyn, a new frontier of opportunities. The streets below filled up with tourists, and he turned up the Walkman, sucking on the stick of smoke that came up sickly sweet into his nostrils. The *chiba* smoke relaxed him and he thought about Jack. The truce was on hold. If the cops could find the Big Uncle's girlfriend that would take suspicion off of him.

But Lucky wasn't surprised. He heard it on the grapevine, about Jack stirring up shit on the streets, rousting the Fuk Chings, busting the Yee Bot. Eventually, Lucky wanted pictures of the undercovers from the Asian Squad but figured it was too soon to play that card. He decided to toss Jack a bone, something to keep him busy, out of the way.

Revelations

Things picked up, but not the way Jack expected.

There was a sniper on the roof of the Smith Houses, which scrambled the SWAT boys out of Headquarters, shut down the Brooklyn Bridge, sucked uniforms out of patrol.

A demonstration at City Hall.

A Terrorist Alert at the Stock Exchange.

Jack was the next man up when the B&E report came into the squadroom, a breaking and entering into a Henry Street apartment, called in by the night janitor.

Apartment 8H was empty, dead air sitting on top of the silk-covered bed. Clothes in the closet, *Dior, Versace, Tahari*, expensive petites left behind. Designer shoes stacked below. Vuitton bags in every configuration.

It wasn't a burglary, more like someone looking for someone, with a vengeance.

The kitchenette was neat, except for the splash of mahjong tiles on the countertop. The refrigerator empty. No garbage in the covered bin.

No personal papers, no pictures. Nothing to put a face to the tenant of the apartment. Nothing to indicate anyone had lived there the last few days.

Jack envisioned a young woman, someone who'd gone on vacation. He went down to the management office, requested the apartment lease.

When *Wah Yee Tom* turned up on the ownership document, Jack knew for sure that the Uncle Four deal had a woman in it, the woman who had the answers he needed.

He snatched up one of the mahjong tiles, the *bak baan*, a white board, a clear slate. He pressed the ivory block inside his fist, squeezing it as if it might yield a clue. He thought of Ah Por again, knew if she could channel anything, the *bak baan* was the cleanest choice, unencumbered by numbers, characters, or symbols. Then he remembered the keys, and started to see how things were coming together. One of the keys fit the apartment lock, but the mechanism was too mashed up for it to turn. When he got down to the lobby, the other two keys worked perfectly. One for the front door, one for the mailbox. He went back in the direction of Mott Street, thinking of Ah Por and Lucky, fearing that time was running out.

Heaven Over Earth

Now she saw rolling hills and fields in broad open valleys, uplands bisected by steep slopes and wretched soils, an unbroken ridge of shale, limestone. The train climbed up from the plateau toward the Alleghenies. Mona closed the blinds and placed the plastic bag on the table, emptied it out.

There were packets of money bundled inside brown laundry paper, a plastic box with columns of gold Chinese Pandas, a small black velveteen pouch.

She took a breath, unzipped the pouch, turned it so that diamonds tumbled into her cupped palm, their brilliance pulsing even in the shadowy daylight behind the blinds, the sight of them freezing her eyes.

Maybe two dozen there, she thought. She poured them back into the pouch, gathered up the rest of the *payback* from the table. *Count it later.* Everything fit perfectly into the empty mahjong case she'd carried the gun in. The case slipped into a neoprene knapsack, all stashed inside the Samsonite. The gun came out of the garment bag, the silencer unscrewed, the magazine ejected. She wrapped all of it in a hand towel, stuffed it into the side compartment of the Rollmaster, and let the light back into the room.

Rugged terrain streaked by, and she could see great lakes far to the north, imagined the Chinese gold coast of Toronto there, considered the possibilities. Seven Chinatowns, newer and cleaner than New York, but lots of Hong Kong Chinese in each. Hip Chings, probably. She watched until the sun began to set behind the mountains. There was no appetite in her stomach and she knew she had to avoid the other passengers.

By nightfall the train had descended into Pittsburgh, then raced west across Ohio and Indiana. She fell asleep in her clothes on the narrow bed, snuggled in beside the knapsack, and awoke fitfully with the first light that filtered in through the blinds.

She brushed her teeth, combed her hair, straightened her clothes. She felt excited and weary at the same time. Coffee and sweet bread came from the dining car. She added XO, finished it off with a chain of cigarettes.

She could keep on the run, she knew, and even be successful

in eluding the police, whose energy and resources would dim after a week or so. But Golo would only be satisfied with the return of the gold and diamonds, or if he had a body with which to account to his superiors for the losses. Golo, she knew, would be harder to evade. Johnny was her wild card, in case Golo got too close. She consulted her jade piece, which suddenly felt cool to her touch.

Beware, it said, *rain follows thunder.*

Move on.

Chicago was a layover where she ducked the passenger lounge in the terminal, keeping the Rollmaster close. Passing the outskirts of Chinatown, she found Wentworth Street, came upon a shopping mall where she filled herself with *jook congee* and *jow gwai,* fried bread. On Archer Boulevard she bought melon cakes from a Chinese bakery. She searched along Canal Street, combed the shops along Twenty-Fourth. At the Oriental Gift Shop she found a Chinese box of dark mahogany, which had the symbolic Double Happiness etched in brass on top, a polished wood rectangle with ornate hinges and a sliding drawer. The small gold stick-on label underneath read "Made in China."

She paid for it with cash.

The next train, the California Zephyr, god of the west wind, would carry her the rest of the way. There were Chinese families aboard; she avoided them.

The SuperLiner crossed the Mississippi, passed the vast bulk and sprawl of prairie lands, tilled and planted with grains, soils of black and red loess. From her window the sky was so big she felt no one would ever catch her.

It was midnight when they arrived in Omaha.

Thirty-six hours out of the Big Uncle's power now, only two things worried her and both were men. Golo would surely come after her, backed by the Hip Chings on both coasts. Johnny would want to keep running, jump the country. *Keep him calm, under control,* she thought. She still needed him, if only for the extra cover he might provide.

The Zephyr surged westward, into the Rockies, through coniferous forests of Ponderosa pine, fir and spruce, sailing through the Divide, passing river canyons and gorges of sedimentary rock. Her window scanned mountain peaks with rolling alpine meadows, timberline savannahs following the Colorado River. A view so striking she had to chase it with brandy to steady herself.

Sell Johnny on the jewelry distributor angle—he'd hook into that. Let him dream about Big Money. Daylight awoke her in Salt Lake City. A soft yellow afternoon.

She kept the rubberized knapsack beside her, made a phone call from the platform.

Lost

Jack couldn't find Ah Por. She wasn't among the old women in the park on Mulberry. When he reached out to them, they provided no clues. He squeezed the mahjong tile inside his pocket, felt his palm get sweaty even as he turned toward Mott Street.

Clues

When Jack reached the intersection, Lucky was already on the corner of Bayard. Lucky jerked his chin sidewise and disappeared into the Wah Rue bookstore. Jack crossed the street, followed him inside.

Lucky patted Jack down, saying "You did good, Jacky boy. Was the money good enough? You need more next time?"

Jack clutched Lucky's probing hand, squeezed the fingers hard. "That's funny, Tat, but I ain't wearing a wire. You owe me, anyway."

Lucky jerked his hand free. "That's right," he said, "and I got something for you."

Jack's eyes narrowed. "Shoot."

Lucky grinned. "Shoot, ha ha, a cop joke, ha?" He paused. "I got the girlfriend."

"Where?" Jack asked with a poker face.

Lucky took him over to the back racks, sliding his hand along the display of ink brushes, wrapping paper, periodicals, until he stopped and yanked out a Hong Kong *Star* magazine. He led Jack through a back exit into a small courtyard lined with *bok choy* crates and garbage cans.

Jack held his tongue while Lucky flipped through the pages. He could hear the rattle and crash of a fan-tan game somewhere below the building.

"Her name's Mona," Lucky said, stopping his finger at In Concert pictures. "Here, looks like this one, Shirley Yip, the singer. You know which one?"

Jack took the magazine, studied the glossies of the singer in a sequined dress, in a black miniskirt, in a hat and wig get-up.

"Thirtysomething," Lucky said. "A real looker, maybe a hooker."

"So where is she?" Jack deadpanned.

"Gone with the wind, Jacky. Only the Shadow knows."

"That's all you got?" Jack was impatient.

Lucky made a face, said, "Hey, I still didn't get nothing. I want the undercovers, identities, names."

"Oh yeah. I'm making a list, checking it twice," cracked Jack.

"No, no, cuz," Lucky wagged his finger, "I don't need no list. I want pictures, know what I'm saying?"

Jack spread the magazine, tore out the pictures. "It's gonna take time," he said softly.

Lucky lit up a Marlboro, spread his hands out and said, "You see me? I got nothing *but* time." And exhaled into Jack's face.

Jack held his stare for a moment, then said, "You know the Twenty-Eight got ripped off the other night?"

"Good for them," Lucky said coolly.

"Took fifty G's out of there. They claim you did it."

"Me?"

"Ghosts, the man said."

Lucky's face changed. "Wasn't my crew," he said.

"Don't know nothing about it, huh?"

Lucky was silent, and stood like that a while. The chatter and curses of the fan-tan game echoed somewhere below them.

"This where it ends for you?" Jack asked. "Gambling? Blood money from poor working suckers?

Lucky let the smoke roll out of his nose. "Hey, Chinese like to gamble. Nobody makes them come down."

Jack sneered. "Yeah they do, *everybody* makes them. Everything they see makes them come down."

"You're bugging out, cousin."

"They want what everyone else's got, and they know money talks."

Lucky laughed small. "Don't get holy, man. It's a Chinaman thing, okay ? You got a beef, go yell at OTB. Shit. It's just a living, man."

"No, it's not. I know how it works. Turn the cash into dope, jewelry, gold. Wash everything through Hong Kong banks. Goes in a big circle, right?"

Lucky flicked the cigarette butt, snuffed it with a twist of his heel.

"What you get over there, Jack? Thirty-five, forty G's with overtime?"

"It's honest money."

"That's what it cost to turn you against people used to be your friends? Against working people who never had no beef with you?"

Jack's face tightened. "We only bust the bad ones, Tat Louie."

"Bullshit. *We* take care of the bad ones. You guys just come for the money, to keep score of the bodies."

Jack glared at Lucky.

Lucky relented. "Maybe not you, Jacky, but cops, you know it. Look, fifty G's, you work for us. Nobody's gotta know. Strictly information stuff. You don't touch nothing dirty."

Jack looked up from the courtyard, saw the oyster-colored sky above the rooftops they used to run across.

"What?" Lucky smirked. "You think you're gonna make sergeant and retire here? Don't kid yourself. I won't make the offer again."

"It's not about money," Jack said.

Lucky sneered.

"It's *all* about money, ain't a damn thing funny."

Chase

Jack sat by the open window in Pa's apartment, studied the magazine pictures and repeated *Mona* quietly, trying to figure her in his head, guessing. Mona, on the run, away from New York City, to somewhere else Chinese where she could disappear, come back in another guise. A major Chinatown, but away from Boston, Philadelphia, Washington. The picture was getting clearer. Los

Angeles, San Francisco, Seattle. From *Lor Saang* she could flee into Mexico. San Francisco, Seattle, she runs north to Canada.

He took a shot of the mao-tai.

Was she still in the country? He thought so, hoped so. Uncle Four would never have allowed her a passport, and the *cheap see*—mistress—wouldn't have had the nerve to troll the underground for fake identification. She probably didn't speak English, so all the arrangements would have to be in Chinese.

He began to list her characteristics on a sheet of paper. *Traveling by plane?* They'd have to cover the airports, just in case. More likely she's in a car, something low key, a bus or train maybe. *Or a boat? Heading east?* Chinese in London, in Amsterdam. He doubted it, didn't figure her to head into bad weather.

Going west, he decided, adding details of Mona to the composite.

She's a Chinese woman, Cantonese, maybe traveling alone, probably traveling light. Thirtysomething, five-foot-two, short hair. Fashionably dressed. Might have booked passage to Mexico or Canada.

He buffed up the profile, made it bilingual, offered a reward, sent it by e-mail via the squadroom computer to the thirty-seven travel agencies in the Chinese Business Directory, to the ninety agencies in Lower Manhattan. Then he thought about covering the funeral, and cleaned his Detective Special while he tried to dope it all out.

Chaos

The Dragon war-wagon cruised to a stop, a huge black sedan with four doors, lurched back out of the crosswalk and sat on the corner of Crosby and Broome.

The three Chinese hard boys inside wore black leather jackets and beat-boy sunglasses. Straight black hair cut to fades. The one with the small ring in his earlobe came out and walked diagonally across the street to where the black Lincoln Continental was parked at the curb. He saw the triple eights on the license plate, saw the car was empty. He crossed back to the Buick and they waited, playing thirteen-card poker and smoking cigarettes. Waited for the six-o-clock rush.

From the Buick they saw the old man approach the black Lincoln, stop at the driver's door. Put the key in the handle. By the time he noticed them closing in, the door had swung open.

Gee Man yanked the keys out and took a step backward, turning to flee. But they were upon him, grabbing at him as he lurched down the street. The keys fell from his hand. He noticed people stopping to watch, the words *go meng*, save me, stuck in his throat. The hard boys brought him down.

"*Matsi!*" he yelled, "What's up?! I have no money."

He did his best to kick out at them in his desperation. He heard himself shouting, like from inside an oil drum, an echo. Pressure building up inside his chest. They were dragging, half-carrying him back toward the car.

"What do you want?" he kept screaming, until the pumping in his heart seized and the lights inside his head went to black.

The Dragon boys dropped Gee Man when he clutched up and foamed from his mouth, left him lying on the cobblestone street, his eyes rolling and flickering, a block from the radio car.

The Buick roared away from the corner, as the evening-rush crowd continued trudging into the sunset.

It was a quarter to eight, almost the end of Jack's shift, when the patrol caught it. Old Chinese man, DOA at Downtown Hospital from a heart attack. Witnesses claimed deceased was attacked by gang kids, who rifled his car.

That could make it a homicide.

Jack took the plate numbers off the report, ran them in the computer—Motor Vehicles, Taxi and Limousine Commission. He crossed into personal overtime when the information floated up on the monitor. Gypsy franchise number *888*. *Jun Yee Wong*. 444 Eighth Avenue. Brooklyn. Didn't match the victim's fact sheet.

Sunset Park. Jack's eyes twitched. About five blocks from his studio, in the Seven-Two Precinct.

Golo bit at his lower lip, tearing tiny pieces of skin from it between the edges of his teeth. He dismissed the gang boys and sat in the dark in the back of the clubhouse.

The Dragons had come back with keys and the driver's address from the car registration, but had left behind a body in the street and many witnesses. He decided not to use them again, the street boys having a way of complicating things. And they may have brought the police into this. He'd have to follow through by himself.

He scanned the papers taken from the triple-eight car. The address was in Brooklyn, around the new Chinatown, he figured. *Wait until nightfall. And bring the Tokarev.*

Clash

Jack buzzed across the Brooklyn Bridge, came up Eighth Avenue until he found the numbers he sought. The street was dead quiet, lined with four-story brick walk-ups that contained a Cantonese herb shop, a Malaysian bookstore, a Maria's Bakery outlet. All closed.

The lock on the door of 444 was loose. No doorbells, no intercom. Jack jiggled the knob. After a moment, sure no one was on the street, he slipped his bankcard behind the lock and popped it.

Went up to 3A.

He listened for a few moments. No sounds from inside. He had started twisting the doorknob when the door swung in, just a crack. *Unlocked.*

Jack put his back to the hall wall, posted his badge, drew his Special. He pushed the door open with his foot, letting hallway light spill into the apartment. He reached in, flicked up the switch inside the door.

The apartment was lit by an incandescent yellow glow. *Empty.* Looked like someone took off in a hurry. Takeout food left behind. Clothing. Unmade bed. A toaster oven, small color TV. Chinese newspapers, racing forms, OTB bet slips.

Jack holstered the revolver.

A dead driver. A missing driver. Another dead body he didn't need. Turn it over to the Seven-Two.

The man appeared suddenly in the doorway, a Chinese man returning Jack's surprise with a nod and a quick scan of the room before he turned to leave.

Six-two, maybe, Jack thought, *tall for a Chinese.* Jack caught him out on the landing, the man turning, his eyes focused on the badge.

"*Ah Sook,*" Jack began, "*uncle . . .*"

The man's hand shot up off his hip, surprising Jack, shoving him sideways. The man shifted as Jack twisted, spun in a small circle and folded down into a cat stance. Caught his breath. He thought he saw a pistol inside the man's coat. The tall man launched two sharp kicks at Jack's head, grunting, forcing him to one side. The hallway closed in on them. Retreating, Jack kept his punches short, Wing Chun style, clipped the taller man under the side of the chin. The man retreated into a crouch then uncoiled in a lashing of Tiger Claw and Iron Fist that drove Jack backward onto the steps.

The man feinted a chop, reached into his coat. Jack reached behind himself for the Special. The man turned to run, a pistol coming out of his coat.

The hallway exploded with gunfire. The tall man ran, fell, rolled down the stairs clutching for the handrail, laying down a barrage of semi-automatic fire that pinned Jack to the stairs, gaining the time he needed for escape.

Before Jack reached the ground floor he heard the squeal of car wheels laying rubber across the avenue. On the street, he could barely make out the taillights fading in the distance. The tall man was gone.

Jack went back to check for bullet casings. There were nine, and also a smear of the tall man's blood on the banister, which he dabbed up with Alexandra's handkerchief. Jack never noticed, until he called in the incident to the Seven-Two, the thin trickle of blood that ran down his left arm and soaked into his shirt cuff.

Drift

The Holiday Inn was a mile from the Greyhound Terminal in Los Angeles, the last stop, just outside of Chinatown. Johnny checked in, tried calling Gee Man again. Nothing. *Probably was out with the car.*

He walked toward Chinatown, flexing the stiffness from his legs, feeling secure enough with the Ruger handy. He bought a Chinese newspaper, had coffee with cold dim sum. Then the picture in his head got huge, the headlines of the newspaper bringing sudden clarity: *Revered Leader Murdered in New York.* A two-page spread with color photographs of Uncle Four.

Mona, Johnny thought immediately.

Flow

Golo rubbed the pungent *teet da jao,* herbal liniment, into the bruise on his elbow until it was stained brown. He leaned over the sink and poured peroxide over the bloody gash on his left forearm, over the strawberry burns on his palm, scraped when he crashed down the stairs ducking the *chaai lo*'s bullets.

Dew ka ma, fucker, he grimaced, applying white adhesive tape over gauze bandages.

He put on a dark suit for the funeral, and wondered how long it would be before the Red Circle inquired about their gold and diamonds.

Questions

The King Sin coffee shop was nicknamed "half ass," as much for the neighborhood dive it was, as for the second-rate oiliness of its home-style cooking. It was a hole-in-the-wall joint, down from the park, on the edge of Ghost Legion territory. Six tables, a counter, a closet-sized short-order grill kitchen, and a cooler full of soda and juice.

Lucky looked inside, swung his gaze around, went in, looking back over his shoulder. *Empty.* The *lo wah kue,* Chinatown old-timer, with the greasy white apron, plucked up his cleaver from the slab of beef in the steamer, nodding with a smirk as Lucky sat down. After a minute, the man served him a plastic plate of *hom g*now, corned beef with boiled cabbage over rice, King Sin's best dish, available nowhere else in Chinatown. Lucky looked out the door to the street, saw the Ghosts in the park, felt the butt of the pistol taped to the underside of the table. He paused and seemed to compose himself for a serious undertaking, then began eating, fork to mouth, his eyes never leaving the door.

Jack stepped in and filled his view, took Lucky's gaze with him back to the small, grimy table.

Lucky put the fork down but Jack spoke first. "I'm looking for a hitter, maybe fifty years old. Big guy, bald head, good with his hands. Shoots a big piece, a Nine. Gotta be from Chinatown."

"Tall man, right?" Lucky knew. "They call him Golo. Enforcer for the Big Uncle. Connected to the *societies* in Hong Kong. *Hung kwun,* bloody stick, all that shit."

"Sounds like you ain't a true believer."

"Red Circle Triad, big deal. It's all hocus-pocus to us. We don't give a shit here. We got the *juice.* Hey, Hong Kong's the fuckin' other side of the world, right?"

Jack nodded. "So where the fuck is he?"

"What do I look like? That guy on TV, the fuckin' Shell Answer-Man?" Lucky spit out. "And not for nothing, Jacky, but don't come here like this next time, okay? It don't look good, us together."

Jack looked behind him, saw the Ghosts in the park, got up. "Tomorrow morning, after the funeral," he said walking out.

"Upstairs."

Dirge

The funeral was an elaborate affair befitting a leader of Uncle Four's stature in the Hip Ching hierarchy. A hundred black limousines shut down traffic for ten blocks all around Chinatown. All the radio-car boys were hired, their Towne Cars and Continentals trailing the Fleetwood flower-wagons, overflowing with wreaths and bouquets from every Chinatown florist.

Through the gray morning rain, the procession was led by a fleet of Cadillac Calais-class cars, which only the Chao Funeral House used, the owner having won the fleet from a heroin importer fronting as a car dealership. The line of cars was wet and dark, shimmering in the drizzle, like a long black snake curling its way through Chinatown. It stopped momentarily at the Hip Ching Association, then at Confucius Towers where Uncle Four had resided. At each stop a funeral band played a plaintive dirge, and groups of Chinese women mourners whimpered together in the same tone, forming a low wail that sounded like the buzzing of bees.

On Mott Street the entire Ghost Legion wore black, two hundred members forming a shadowy wedge under the ominous sky. Local residents stood with their heads huddled together under umbrellas, like a sea of black bobbing mushrooms.

Fox News set up alongside Channel Seven, amid a phalanx of photographers from the dailies, who were perched on top of folding stepladders. The Federal boys—DEA, FBI, Treasury—hid openly in a brown Ford van with blacked-out windows, cameras whirring behind them. Conspicuous agents trying to look inconspicuous.

Jack stood on the corner of Bayard Street behind black sunglasses and watched as the last chapter of the old man's life unfolded.

What about the girlfriend? He flexed against the bandage the hospital had patched over his bicep, felt a dull stinging burn. The trail was twisting, getting colder, and he began to feel like he was losing it.

From translucent sky came a fine mist falling upon the scatter of umbrellas.

Then Lucky stepped out from among the Legion, blowing smoke, his sunglass eyes watching Jack scoping the procession. Lucky felt their eyes meeting, even behind the dark lenses, knew the cops were plodding around searching for leads. He laughed inside his head. *Somebody caps a big shot, they gonna hang around?* He scanned the Legion, an impressive show of solidarity even though he knew some people suspected a double cross. *The truce?* Up in the air. Until a perpetrator turned up.

He turned his attention back to Jack.

Jack was gone.

Now with horns blaring, the end of the long black procession cleared the red signal at the end of Mott Street and cruised out of sight.

Lucky crushed out his cigarette and left the street, a tide of black draining with him.

Warnings

Lucky stepped onto the Mott Street rooftop, Jack behind him.

"A long time since I been up here," Lucky said, scanning the city of rooftops, a cloud shadow passing beneath the wet sky. "So what the fuck is happening with you? How's the old man?"

"Buried him two weeks ago," Jack answered.

"Too bad how shit happens." Lucky frowned. "My old man, be better off dead. Fuckin' drunk waste of life."

They avoided each other's eyes.

"Anyway," Lucky spat out, "what's up? You didn't get me up here for old time's sake."

Jack saw the Brooklyn Bridge, the Lower Manhattan skyline. He said, without looking at Lucky, "You did me a solid. I owe you, so listen good to what I'm going to say."

Lucky shrugged his shoulders, listened.

"This is some heavy shit you're involved with. You think you're going to last forever? Remember Kid Taiwan? Mongo Jo? Riki Baby? All the *dailo*, big brothers, before you? They all thought they were big-time, like no one could touch them."

The Seaport, Brooklyn in the distance.

"They're all doing Federal time, Tat. Chinaman time. Everybody-looking-to-fuck-you-over time. Time you get out, your dick will be too old to work."

He watched as Lucky smirked, flared up a cigarette, said, "If you're so concerned, just drop a dime, but let me know when they're coming for me."

Jack's eyes settled on the monolithic hulk of the Tombs Detention Facility.

"Can't do that, Lucky," he said in a voice like cool steel, "even if I knew."

Lucky mixed his words with cigarette smoke. "Don't bullshit me, man. You know the deal. The way you set up the Fuk Chings with the Feds, I know you got the juice."

Stroking me, Jack thought, running his knuckles across his eyebrows.

"Just get out of the life before they come. Get out now. Yesterday. That's all I can tell you and I won't say it again."

"Thanks for nothing," Lucky sneered, "but I'll take my chances." He came close enough for the smoke accompanying his words to touch Jack's face.

"When Wing died, I learned two things. One, the only way to get anything is to take it. The only way you get respect is through power. Those who don't have power get out of Chinatown or they stay slaves. Second, the cops don't make a difference. They're just *gwailo* micks and guineas strolling the streets like they own the fuckin' place, call everybody *chingchong wingwong*, get a good laugh, right? You know it. They goof off for eight hours, write a few traffic tickets, then slide to the bar and swap Chinaman jokes. You remember, don't you? *Cat fried lice? Tomaine lo mein? Hahaha.* Fuckin' white bullneck *mamalukes* too dumb to do college end up as cops. Well, fuck *that,* and fuck *them. We* own the streets, not them. See, to me, to the boys, Chinatown is our life. Not a job, not a paycheck. Every minute, every day, we're here to stay."

Jack let him run on, enjoying it.

"Outside of here, we can't be nothing. But here, we can make enough money to be kings."

"Or die trying, right?"

"Try *not* to die trying," Lucky snapped back, crushing the cigarette into the roof wall. "You got a bug up your ass or what? You think you're Batman? Do good? Fight the gangs? Ha. Remember, *I* got even for Wing. Not you. Not the cops. My boys took the Yings off the street. Forever. You know it, we took over."

Jack nodded. "Yeah," he said. "I know you did. So what? You became just like them, the punks that put the knife into Wing's heart. Just like them, you rip off your own people, and you deal poison to the junkies so they keep coming around fucking with our neighborhood. You brother-up with everything we used to hate."

Lucky did a slow circle around Jack. "When the fuck did you become Charlie Chan? You think it's going to be different because you're Chinese? That people here are going to give you more face? Respect you? You're part of the same corrupt shit, Jacky. The Blue Gang. NYPD Blue. Read the papers. Cops dealing drugs. Cops taking money. Cops fucking over anyone who ain't white. You heard of Rodney King? That badge don't make you no better, brother. You know the game. I get busted, half an hour I'm back on the street. You think you've stopped something because someone got arrested? Wake up, Jacky. See my side of things."

He stooped, matched up to Jack's eyes. "Chinaman cop. First sign of trouble, you'll be the first guy they give up. So what's with the cop thing? A steady paycheck? Trying to live large on chump change?"

Jack was silent, annoyance crossing his face, wondering how high the price would go. He leaned in, said, "*Honest* work, Tat. Something you wouldn't know about. Sure I know you think you're living large. Big-time bullshit gangsta hype. Doesn't your neck hurt looking over your shoulders all the time? I've seen you on the corner, shuffling, got your back to the wall. You sleep with one eye open. You got your gat under the pillow and jump when the phone jangles. You *like* living like that, *big time?* Living *large?*"

Lucky just smiled. "Come over to my side," he said. "Let's deal.

What makes it work for you? Cash money don't move you? How about fresh pussy every week? You didn't go *gaylo* on me didja? Jewelry, fine clothes, a new ride? Can't touch it."

Jack frowned disdain into the corners of his mouth. "*Won't* touch it, brother," he said.

Lucky rolled on. "Like I said before, you don't have to do anything dirty. Just information, identification. Like that." A pause, then Lucky's eyes gleam sharp with an epiphany. "I get it. You can't admit what you want. All this brings some kinda dishonor to your cop thing. Okay, so go *this* way. I give you some inside dope, schemes and scams from the secret societies, who the players are, how it all works. You help the Feds take them down, be the big *hero*. You get promoted up the kazoo. Me, I don't care about that international I-Spy stuff. You give me information to protect my boys, and take out the local competition. I get them before they get me. That's all. You go up. I go *large*. Neither one of us gets trapped."

"Sure," Jack said finally. "Yeah, I'll think about it."

"But don't mistake the offer for weakness," Lucky said warily. "You wouldn't be the first cop on our pad. Not even the first *Chinese cop*."

Jack grinned, wondering which *other* Chinese cops were dirty? "Well, considering that this offer comes from a guy who's got all his cash stashed in a deposit box because he can't use the banks, and who's got everything leased or borrowed because his name ain't worth a shit, tell me why I should respect this offer?"

Lucky leaned in closer. "Because I know the way this game works. The same way I got the Yings out, you know I can make it happen. The information I get you will make you a lieutenant, a captain. You'll be retired before you're forty. With a cop pension. Retire like a big hero. Don't die broke and penniless like your old man, brother."

Jack stepped back. "Like I said, you should get out yesterday.

You're only top dog until the next hungry Fuk Ching kid pops you just to make his bones."

Fuck you tugged up the corners of Lucky's mouth, contempt filling his eyes.

Jack looked east. "I'll think about it," he repeated.

"Well, take yourself a good serious think, man," Lucky chilled. "Because I ain't making this offer again. So don't bother coming back with a wire the next time we talk."

Their eyes battled a moment.

"And don't tell me you *like* being out there, dealing with the scummy low-life scabs of the city for sucker pay."

Lucky left Jack there, walked back into the shadow of the stairwell. The roof door slammed as he turned, went down the flights of stairs.

At the bottom landing, he looked back up to the skylight of the roof, didn't see any sign of Jack, frowned, and switched off the tape machine strapped to his groin.

Discovery

The woman agent in the Golden Lotus Travel Service tapped into the keyboard, scrolled through electronic data on the color computer monitor.

"We had someone come in last week," she said to Jack in Cantonese, "a woman who fits the description."

"Last week?" Jack kept his cool, stared over her shoulder at the digital waves.

"Might have been Thursday or Friday. I had the weekend off and only saw your fax message this morning."

"What did she look like?"

"She wore black, short hair. Never took her sunglasses off."

Her eyes flickered. "Here it is."

Jack breathed through his nose, measured his breaths.

"It wasn't Mexico. Or Canada. She booked one seat one way to Los Angeles. Greyhound Bus. The Holiday Inn near Chinatown."

"Under what name?"

"J. Wong," she answered.

"When?" Jack asked as she tore off the printout and gave it to him.

"Should have arrived today."

Jack smiled, thanked her.

"The Department will be in touch with you regarding the reward," he said. She appeared happy as he left her little office.

When he got back to the 0-Five, the phone on Jack's desk was ringing, a call the switchboard patched through from the Translation Project downstairs. The voice was Cantonese, a woman speaking with a Hong Kong accent.

"The man you are looking for was the Big Uncle's driver. Jun Yee 'wong jai,' kid wong. Wong," she repeated.

Jack tried to stall her for a trace but she repeated the name once more and hung up. *JunYee Wong,* he realized, *the missing radio driver from Brooklyn.* The circle was shrinking.

Downstairs, they got a partial area code off the call. 303. Best guess was somewhere in Colorado. *Colorado?*

A crank call? *The mistress. Then who was enroute to Los Angeles?*

Jack decided to install a caller ID device, his head piecing together scattered impressions of a missing woman. His eyes ate up the travel agent's printout before he made the call.

The long-distance male voice was brusque, efficient, no-nonsense. He said, "Like, this is LA, *buddy*. We're five minutes outside of

Chinatown so, yes, we've got lots of Chinese men, and women, in lots of our rooms. I can't give you that kind of information over the telephone."

Jack identified himself for the second time.

"Yes," the voice continued, "NYPD. So you say, but on this end I don't know you from Joe Blow citizen. You get my point of view?"

"Can't you even confirm if it's a Chinese man, or woman, in that room?"

"Can't do it. Suppose I tell you and someone gets killed?"

"Suppose you *don't* tell me and someone gets killed?" Jack growled.

"Not my problem."

"Thanks for nothing." Jack slammed the phone down. He considered reaching out to LAPD, but worried about spooking the fugitives, losing his shaky leads to the mistress and the driver.

Then he heard the transmission coming over the static on the squadroom radio, crackling something about Major Case coming in on the Uncle Four killing. Bringing in the Big Dicks, sliding him into the background.

He knew that was how it worked. *It's not that the Fifth Squad can't be trusted.* Operations wanted more experience, older dicks from Manhattan South.

Jack tuned out the thought, unofficial as it was, and started considering the time difference versus the flight time to Los Angeles. Then the squadroom door swung open.

Distance

The old men entered the storefront at 8 Pell in single file. They removed their hats, sat down, caught their breaths. Five gray-haired men looking out on the street where they lost their youth.

The *hung gwun*, enforcer, Triad red-pole rank, had requested their presence here in the clubhouse instead of meeting formally at 20 Pell, to save the old gentlemen three flights of stairs, and to ensure the privacy of the meeting.

Golo came around the partition and quickly offered his respects to them. He spoke quickly, to the point.

"There is a woman involved in this. Perhaps some of you have seen her?"

A pause as the old men pretended to search their minds.

"Alert your secretaries. You must offer a reward for information, contact all Chinese travel agents, but keep her out of the newspapers."

"A bounty?" one of the elders asked.

"If you prefer, Uncle, to put it that way," Golo answered respectfully before continuing.

"You must contact your counterparts in Los Angeles, San Francisco, Vancouver. Also, all East Coast Chinatowns. They must send people to cover the main airports. But don't neglect the bus terminals, the trains, the hotels and motels nearest our communities."

The old men paid due attention, respect owed to Golo for his efforts in the aftermath of the murder of their leader. They understood. The eldest rose from his wooden chair, the others followed, nodding, putting on their hats.

Golo gave them sheets of paper with Mona's and Johnny's

profiles worded in Chinese, like an invitation. He followed them out of the storefront and watched them go down the street into the double doors of Number 20. His watch showed late afternoon, and he wondered how far away Mona, and his cache, had gotten.

The Liner slipped down into the Valley.

Utah passed in the darkness, craggy headlands, rolling plains under moonlight. Mona slept a troubled sleep, a nightmare with ghost coolies, bloody pickaxes, Chinese women and children screaming, murdered in the night.

The train sliced through the flat vastness of desert, hot and bone dry, the vistas so sunny she put the Vuarnets back on. The desolate beauty caught her. Nevada flashing by made her feel she could start forgetting New York.

She napped until there was a stop at Reno; the sunshine fell onto the desert. The Sierra Nevada rolled up, then dropped from granite into a fertile sunlit valley on the western shore.

The California Zephyr drifted to a stop in Oakland before noon.

Mona waited until the Chinese families passed her compartment, then emerged and fell in behind them. No one would be able to tell she was traveling alone.

Seventy-two hours from New York, she briskly crossed the platform, the Hermès scarf moving now, pulling the Rollmaster on a march through the Bay Area Rapid Transit system in the direction of Chinatown.

Pursuit

The Chinese lowriders in the red Trans Am wore tight perms and biker sunglasses, faded denim jeans and baggy shirts opened to gold bar-link chains around their thick necks. The grumble of the car died as the three young men inside walked out under the hot L.A. sun and crossed the parking lot, jostling each other, into the Holiday Inn.

Johnny stayed in his hotel room, rereading the newspaper. Uncle Four's funeral, biggest in Chinatown history. The Chings were going to be hot, seeking Mona, Johnny realized, and L.A. didn't seem like the place to stop. His mood swung, he readjusted his identity from partner to *accomplice*. He'd scored the gun and that tied him in.

Partners, she'd said, the word ringing in his ears. Yeah, he thought, partners *in crime*.

He came to a news item about a dead radio-car driver, which stopped his heart a beat. *Gee Man, a heart-attack victim, dead near the Lincoln.* In that moment he felt the weight of their pursuit, how deadly serious they were, after him also.

He went to the lobby and rented a car, paid cash in advance. When he drove it off the lot he passed a Trans Am, blood red, parked off the main entrance. Like a bleeding shark with dark window eyes. It reminded him of New York.

He parked the rental car outside his room window, nervously came back to the lobby. There was a crowd of Japanese tourists in Hawaiian shirts, a group of Chinese Kiwanis. A Cub Scout pack.

He thought he spotted some perm cuts or sunglasses that could be L.A. Ching boys. He didn't think they saw him, but he didn't feel so safe anymore.

Slipping back inside the room, he checked the Ruger, got whiskey from the honor bar, sucked the little bottles down while waiting for Mona's call.

Moves

The afternoon was sunny when Mona descend from the Thruway bus in San Francisco, flagged a cab, gave the driver a slip of paper that said San Rema Motel.

The San Rema Motel was a converted warehouse at the fringe of Chinatown where it stretched into North Beach and rose into Russian Hill.

Mona took a room on the middle floor, facing the courtyard so she could see who was entering, so she could exit up or down with ease.

The landings which connected the two sections of the motel gave onto numerous exits at the front and back of the complex. She checked the three best routes: from the landings, from the roof, the garage. Stockton Street was the main north-south thoroughfare, leading south to the airport, or north toward the Bay.

She lit a cigarette and took a long drag. *Stockton*, she was thinking, *would be the way to go*. She changed into a gray sweatsuit and sneakers, took a bus down to the Business District.

As in New York she found a travel agency that was American but employed a *jook sing*, American-born Chinese girl, who spoke enough Cantonese to be of help.

Two blocks outside Chinatown she found a convenience store where she purchased a sheet of *gay pay ji*, plain brown wrapping paper, packing tape, a black marker.

At the San Rema, Room Service delivered a fifth of brandy. Mona nestled the Titan into the Chinese box, was pleased with the fit, then reassembled it with the silencer, the little clip of bullets. She took a taste of the brandy, caught her breath again. Put everything into the Rollmaster. It was almost two, and she thought about calling Johnny, to be sure of what was going on with him. She put on her Vuarnets and went out onto the sunny slope behind the motel.

On the hilly sidewalk, outside a Chinese restaurant, she inserted the phone card, made the call.

"Where are you?" Johnny asked.

She heard the edge on his voice. "*Saam Fansi,*" she said calmly. *Play it straight with him.* "The San Rema Motel." *She still needed him.*

There was surprise in his voice now and she announced quickly, "I am speaking to you from an outside phone. I only have time to say this once, so listen carefully."

She imagined him nodding yes, grabbing for pen and paper so he wouldn't miss a word.

"Get yourself a car. Wait until night and drive up." She paused for effect. "I need you here" *Selling him the plan, the dream.* "We're partners, remember. I'm setting up in the jewelry business."

"Jewelry?" he asked.

"But I can't talk about it here. Write this down. San Rema Motel. San, like in mountain." *Way mah,* unnecessary trouble, he was hearing. San Ray-Ma. 100 Stockton, see *dork den,* he was hearing it phonetically. "Room 3M. Wait for dark, make sure no one follows you."

She hung up and adjusted the phone card, then her eyes scanned the number on the torn swatch of Chinese newspaper. *Call New York,* she thought, as she waited through the audio response.

* * *

It was 9 a.m. L.A. time when Golo, calling from New York, got hold of Fifth Brother in the Ching association at Wilshire and Yellow.

"No need to waste words, brother," he said. "Room 3M at the Holiday Inn in Chinatown. There's a man, maybe a man and a woman."

"What do you desire? "

"Follow them, do nothing else."

"Done. What else?"

"I need a gun. Nine-millimeter. When I arrive."

"I'll send the *leng jai,* the punk boys. One of them will pack for you."

"My respects to Seventh Uncle, brother."

"Respects all around."

Golo hung up, and left the clubhouse, went toward Mulberry, where the last of the incense filtered out of the Wah Sang funeral house onto the street and made bittersweet the spirit of the night.

Betrayal

The two bulls from Internal Affairs Division surprised Jack, two big white cops with neat crewcuts and eyes like steel rivets. The captain introduced them, Rob Hogan, Paul DiMizzio. Jack watched quietly as Hogan spoke first.

"Detective, can you explain why we have you on videotape going down to Number Nine Mott Street? Why P.O. Jamal Josephs confirms a subsequent meeting in a bookstore with a known Chinatown gang leader? And why the DEA has you on a bug offering to deliver confidential department information?"

Jack was speechless a moment, his heart trembling during the questions, absorbing the shock and surprise.

"If you have that on tape, you should know I was investigating the Uncle Four shooting."

"And you got shot yesterday, am I correct?"

"Yes," Jack said. "It was only a graze."

"You got shot because of the investigation?"

"I'm not sure it's connected."

"What have you come up with in your investigation?"

"Nothing concrete. I'm working some angles." There was a pause. The men shook their heads, frowning.

"With due respect," Jack said, "the department expects me to solve a crime in seventy-two hours because I'm Chinese?"

The bent-nosed partner, DiMizzio, stepped forward.

"You knew it was illegal to go down into that basement?" he challenged.

"Not in the course of an investigation—"

"Bullshit, Yu. You went down at midnight, twice. That's after your shift and on your own time."

"Yeah, because there's a freeze on overtime, otherwise—"

"Public Morals Division has it under surveillance. Were you aware of that?"

Jack shook his head.

"You might have compromised several ongoing investigations, besides associating with known members of Chinese organized crime."

"He was someone I knew from the neighborhood."

"You saying you have a snitch in the Ghost Legion?"

"I didn't say that."

"That's too bad, he could have been helpful."

Hogan, never taking his eyes off Jack, said, "Yeah, we know all about Tat Louie and his punk-ass bullshit. Gambling. Drugs. Extortion. Another On Yee wannabe. Yeah, we know he was shit deep on the Peking Haircut Case. Nine years ago. Remember that?"

Jack remained quiet, staring back, thinking of Wing.

DiMizzio said, "Three Wah Ying gang members butchered in that barbershop on Hester? Stabbed. Shot. Had their dicks cut off?"

"Yeah," Jack answered. "Never caught anyone, did you?"

"No," said Hogan. "The case is still open, but we know Tat was involved. And you two were friends then, correct?"

"I was in the army then."

Hogan smirked, said, "Funny how the Ghosts walked in and took over after that. Never saw another Wah Ying anywhere."

Jack smirked back. "Yeah, well, the world spins like a wheel. What goes around, comes around."

DiMizzio glowered. "What's that? Chinese philosophy? Or are you condoning murder?"

"Just like I said," Jack repeated. "What goes around, comes around. What's your beef? It's my fault you don't know how to close a case?"

"Maybe you know more than you're saying," Hogan snapped. "Maybe you were involved."

"Maybe you should go fuck yourself," Jack barked.

"Tough guy, huh?" Hogan scowled. "We're going to keep an eye on you."

"Yeah, the way you guys keep an eye on things, I know I got nothing to worry about."

DiMizzio moved closer. "Smartass, worry about this. A lawyer for the Fuk Ching Association has filed a complaint of harassment, claiming you tried to shake them down. What do you say to that?"

"Bullshit. An idiot could see through that."

The captain flashed a look of disgust as Hogan closed the interview.

"We're suspending you, Detective, pending further investigation. Surrender your gun to the captain, and keep yourself available to the department."

Jack handed over the Colt wordlessly as they watched him, then went to clean out his desk, his mind boiling. *This is the way they slide me out?* The captain wouldn't back him, a four-month transfer cop he'd never really got to know. *Inscrutable.* Jack knew it.

DiMizzio and Hogan skulked away. The captain banged into his office and slammed the door behind him.

They had betrayed him, after all the hard work he'd put in, Jack fumed. They were going to kill the investigation, let him go down on charges while suspended.

They, they, they. He was unsure where to assign blame, direct his anger, for the shapeless, silent conspiracy of cops and politics all around him.

Fuck them, he thought, he'd figure out his PBA moves when the formal charges came down.

He pulled his knapsack from the locker, was turning to go when the phone rang.

He recognized the woman's voice. "Jun Yee Wong is at the Holiday Inn, Los Angeles," she said. "Chinatown."

I know this, he began thinking.

The caller ID flashed (415) 444-8888.

"Room 3M. He will be gone when night falls." The phonecall ended, he heard the dial tone.

Jack ran the area code until it stopped at San Francisco; a woman from the Bay City sending him off to Los Angeles. But if he pulled in the SFPD, he knew everyone might disappear.

He toted the knapsack out of the stationhouse and jumped into the first radio car on line at Confucius Plaza.

"LaGuardia," he said, "and push it."

East To West

At the airport, Jack flashed his memorial gold badge from the Detectives' Endowment Association, a black mourning band hiding the letters DEA, with added distraction from his photo ID, which was prominently displayed on the flap of the badge case. The security man at the gate checked the identification card, matched the photo to Jack's face, never suspecting Jack was under suspension. The off-duty Glock rested snugly in the holster in Jack's waistband, and quietly slipped onto the plane with him.

The flight out of LaGuardia had been delayed an hour, and when he arrived at LAX, it was already in the thick of the evening rush. He reached the Holiday Inn too late to catch the guest in 3M, but the motel clerk identified Johnny Wong from the Taxi and Limousine Commission license photo, said he'd left midafternoon, his room key was in the return slot.

"He rented a car," the clerk said.

Jack cursed quietly. Johnny had had a few hours head start already.

"It was a Ford compact." He gave Jack the license plate number.

Jack knew he would patch it along to the highway patrol, but he figured the Ford compact would be heading north. To San Franscisco. He punched up San Francisco Bell on his cell phone and identified himself, requested a phone location. Then he caught a return limo back to LAX.

Go

Johnny cruised the coastal highway north, stayed under the speed limit. To his left a gray mist blended the sky with ocean, laying down a curtain of fog. Below him the whitecap surf was a green-blue blur far under the concrete highway. He cranked down the window, took a breath. Night was too far off, and he had gotten spooked, jumping the gun. San Francisco was maybe nine hours away, with the wind buffing his face. He thought he could be there by morning.

A red muscle car appeared, a dot in his rearview mirror, a few cars back. As he noticed it, it dropped back, disappeared. He wondered if it was the same car he'd spotted at the hotel.

Find Mona, the woman who'd escorted death and fear into his life, *try to get some straight answers.*

The road twisted toward the tree line above the mountains of Big Sur. Traffic thinned out. The light faded to night and all the cars looked black and shapeless in the mirrors. The ocean crashed below in the darkness and he couldn't tell anymore if anyone was following him.

The highway flew by with the smell of salt air. He put on the radio for background, pop music; the reception cut in and out. He thought of Mona, and the last time their bodies had touched.

Stop

It was dark when Golo's phone jangled, Fifth Brother's low boys calling from their car at an all-night takeout shack outside Salinas.

"He's stopped for coffee," they said. "Looks like we're heading for San Francisco."

"I'm on my way," Golo said.

Fog

The fog was cool and wet as it rolled up Grant Avenue near the highway, then slipped back down Jackson, past the phone booth outside the Pagoda Restaurant where Jack stood watching the evening settle over the Bay. He had just caught the 7:10 out of LAX and was hoping Wong *jai* was going to turn up in San Francisco. The circle was closing, and he knew Mona was inside it somewhere.

He sat in the rented car, took out the magazine pictures and his Glock, loaded fifteen hollow-points into the clip and watched the phonebooth. He called the agency on the cell phone and put out a bulletin on Johnny's rental car, wondered where it'd turn up. Midnight passed and no one came down Jackson. He drained his second coffee and pondered his next move, sitting in the hushed night, waiting through the mist for the first light of day.

Shadow

The red muscle car with black-tinted windows followed at a distance as the highway signs ran from Redwood City, San Mateo, Burlingame, to San Francisco. The unseen passengers watched Johnny's compact rental go north, then east toward the Bay. The rental car was moving slow and easy, and that suited them just fine.

Johnny felt as if he was being followed again. But when he checked his mirrors he saw nothing suspicious, just the normal lights of night traffic queuing up behind him, even as he turned into the San Rema.

Nobody followed him in, and he told himself he was just being overly cautious. He checked the address he'd scribbled on the piece of memo paper from the Holiday Inn.

Then he parked the car in the space nearest the exit.

The Trans Am powered around the complex and rolled into the parking lot from the back access road. The engine idled and one of the low boys came out carrying a cell phone in his hand, keeping to the shadows as he followed Johnny into the courtyard. He watched Johnny go up to the middle landing, turn left toward the third door in the row, knock on it.

There was a long pause, words spoken low from Johnny's mouth. The low boy brought the *daai gor daai*—cellphone—to his ear, tapped into the keypad a direct pager redial.

Then he backed away toward the red car, scoping Johnny, and waiting for Golo Chuk.

Lies

Mona hadn't expected Johnny. She was surprised at the knock on her door. She kept quiet, holding her breath, calming her heartbeat, moving toward the pistol in the Samsonite.

"It's *me,* Wong *jai,*" the voice said.

She realized what had gone wrong; the cops had failed. She fought the urge to flee. He knocked again. She watched him through the peephole and gathered herself, playing it cool, letting him in.

"You got here fast," she said, pouring him a drink.

"As fast as I could," he answered, tired out from the long drive.

"Rest up, we're safe here," she said. "For now."

Johnny lay down on her bed and began to wonder what was going to happen next, but the brandy was tuning him out. She turned off the lights and, like that, he was asleep instantly.

Mona plotted through the darkness. *Wait until daybreak.* Then she'd call from the outside again. The same setup, only the location had changed. *Curses on the police, practically being handed the fugitive, they still let him slip away.* She knew Johnny was edgy so she'd have to convince him to stay put, for a couple of days at least. Her mind was spinning, the ideas spiraling in her head.

Waiting

Daylight washed over the Bay, a serene picture. Jack could see activity over toward Portsmouth, old folks practicing Tai Chi. A few people, some schoolchildren, passed, strolling down Jackson.

He checked his watch, wondered who would show at the phone stand, wondered if he wasn't wasting his time. There was nothing else he could do, he decided. His cop future hung on a woman's phone call.

Arrival

Golo deboarded the redeye flight from New York, hustled a cab to the San Rema Motel and found the red Trans Am. When the black window powered down he smelled the rush of marijuana smoke, saw the low boys with their gold chains.

"*Chuk sook*," one of them said respectfully, "Seventh Uncle, the man went into Room 3M."

"You have something for me?" Golo asked, disdain in his voice.

The low boy handed him a Star nine-millimeter, said, "There's a full clip of Black Talons. You have to cock it first."

"I know how it works," Golo snapped, disgusted at the veiny redness of their eyes. He remembered the fuckup with the gang boys in New York, didn't want trouble or witnesses this time around.

"You can go," he said, dismissing them. "My respects to Fifth Brother."

The Trans Am growled away, disappearing into morning traffic. Golo felt for the handcuffs and knife in his pocket and chambered a round into the Star.

He spat onto the sidewalk and started toward room 3M.

Mona kept her eyes on Johnny, who lay crashed in her bed, and quietly backed her way out of the room, pulling the door shut with a small metallic click. She straightened her sunglasses and followed the landing down to the courtyard.

Jack fought the heaviness in his eyes, rubbed his temples.

A woman was coming down the hill, wearing a gray jogging suit and sunglasses, a black bag under her arm. When she got halfway down someone else appeared at the top, a tall man with his hands pressed down inside his jacket pockets. He followed her, keeping at a distance.

Something vaguely familiar about him, Jack thought.

The woman stopped at the phone booth, fumbled with a square of paper.

Jack brought out the glossies from the Hong Kong magazine.

Short haircut. She lowered the sunglasses a moment, carefully pressing the phone buttons. *Looked like Shirley Yip?* She was on the phone only a minute.

Jack decided there was enough of a resemblance, then the tall man came through the parking lot behind the Pagoda Restaurant, his face taut and grim in a way Jack recognized from the shootout in Sunset Park.

The woman spotted the tall man almost immediately while he was still a half block away. She dropped the phone, started running back up the hill.

Jack exited the car holding the Glock as the man followed her. They ran two blocks uphill and went toward a motel building on the next corner, Stockton, as Jack chased up the hill after them.

BLANG!

Johnny's eyes snapped open, saw Mona at the door, breathless.

"What?" he asked, rising up from the bed.

"Trouble," she gasped.

He grabbed his vest, the Ruger. "What happened?"

"Someone must have followed you." Desperation showed in her eyes.

He went to the door, while she snatched up the Rollmaster, and pointed at her to hush. He listened for a long moment as she squinted out the window toward Stockton, getting her bearings. Her mind clicking, *These dogs will not stop me*. Not a sound outside.

"If we get split up," she whispered, "we meet at the Empress, by Chinatown. In the lobby by the telephones." Johnny nodded agreement.

Mona took the little automatic out of the Rollmaster, jerked her chin at the door. *Nothing can stop me now*.

"Let's go," she said.

Jack followed Golo into the motel complex, across the courtyard, trailed him one landing below as he climbed toward the third level. Jack snapped back the action on the Glock, the hollowpoints lining up in the chamber. Took the safety off as he ascended.

Golo, inching his way onto the third landing, listened for noises. A door opened a crack, then he saw the gunbarrel come out. He was backing up when he fired, the concussion from the high-impact Talons deafening him. He rolled back around the bend of the landing and heard footsteps below. *Deeew!*, the *chaai lo*—cop— who'd almost bagged him in Brooklyn.

He fired three rounds in Jack's direction. Everybody froze between landings.

"Police!" Jack yelled. He heard the sudden snapping of locks behind hallway doors. "Throw your guns down!"

Johnny let loose three deafening magnum rounds, sprinting up the stairs toward the rooftop, Mona at his back. Golo dashed up after them.

"Shit!" Jack cursed, following them up. He knew with this much firepower someone was bound to drop out of the deal.

And someone was going back to New York with him.

Fire

Jack slammed out of the exit door onto the rooftop, the Glock held out in front of him, in a combat stance. He saw Golo ahead to his right, lining up his sights on Johnny. Mona, split left of Johnny, was ahead of them, moving toward the far end of the rooftop.

"*Mo yook!*" Jack roared, Freeze! He fixed a bead on Golo.

Then he saw it happening in his mind's eye—the heads ahead of him turning, distracted for just a split second, and the firecracker popping of Mona's little gun chipping brick off the wall above him.

He snapped off four rapid shots at Golo, ducking and sprinting toward Johnny, swinging his gunfire in an arc between them as they ran. Mona was almost at the far rooftop exit.

Jack kept firing, chasing them as the circle of bullets tightened around the two men.

Johnny clutched at his leg, emptying the Ruger as he fell,

blasting at Golo, who was turning to go after Mona. Golo fell out of the deal. Jack pegged two shots at Mona as she stepped behind the closing exit door.

The door slammed shut. Then there was silence as Jack swiveled his Glock from Golo on the ground to Johnny, with his blasted leg. The shootout hadn't lasted ten seconds, it was still singing in his ears.

Jack saw Golo, very dead, a nickel-sized hole in his right temple, the exit impact reducing the left side of his face to bloody cartilage and shreds of white slimy muscle. With handcuffs dangling off his back hip, Jack put his foot across Golo's wrist and kicked the Star out of the dead man's hand. The hardened horror of it froze Jack a moment. Then he snatched for his handcuffs.

He cuffed Johnny to Golo and sprinted toward the roof door behind which Mona had disappeared.

Flight

Mona latched the door, headed toward the stairs.

A barrage of 9mm Silvertip hollow-points punched through the sheet metal door, crashed and spun through the Rollmaster, ripping out its steel grips, pieces of plastic spraying from it.

Mona felt stinging in her leg but was too pumped up to stop. She dashed down the stairs, exiting onto Stockton before she realized the blood flowing down her leg was her own. It had soaked a black line down the pantleg of her sweatsuit. She rushed down the street.

An old De Soto taxi turned onto Stockton as the light turned green.

The rooftop exit door was locked, bolted from inside. Jack ran back to the other exit door to the roof, leading down onto Jackson Street.

Mona climbed into the blue-and-white cab and it rolled east, toward the Bay. She got a Kotex pad from the busted piece of Samsonite, pushed it under the elastic waistband of her sweatpants and held it over the shallow punctures in her thigh.

Destiny, she thought, *jing deng*.

She rolled the window down, saw the Bay rushing by and held her face into the wind.

By the time Jack reached Stockton there was nothing to see, only the taillights of traffic moving away, north and south. She could have gone either way.

He cursed and shook his head, and then went back for *Jun Yee*, Johnny *wong jai wong*.

Return

Jack's life was in limbo, even as Major Case cops at LaGuardia took custody of Johnny, handcuffed to the wheelchair they rolled him away in.

Jack knew they'd expect a report, paperwork details, even though he was still officially suspended. He was crashing in the cab back to Sunset Park when he saw the discarded *Newsday*. An item about a burning body leaped out at him. He fought the numbing shock long enough to read it.

State Troopers from Dutchess County, alerted by campers, had discovered the burning body of a Chinese national dumped in a wooded area of the hamlet, sixty-two miles north of New York City. They suspected he had been murdered in Chinatown. The body showed signs of having been beaten and strangled. They'd found Chinese-language papers in his pocket.

DNA samples had been taken, and the Dutchess County Medical Examiner's office had sent evidence down to the 0-Five for assistance.

Closure

When Jack awoke it was night and chilly in the Brooklyn apartment. He dressed and rousted up a cab to Chinatown, went directly to the caller ID linked to his office tape machine. The woman's last message was locked to the location of the phone stand on Jackson, as he expected. It said, "Jun Yee did it. He was in love with me. He thought he was trying to protect me. I begged him not to, but he was crazy jealous. He could not hold the anger inside. Yes, Jun Yee killed the old man. So I could be free. He is in *Saam Faansi* . . ." He listened until the tape filled with traffic noise, and the operator ended the call. He left the tape machine, went down to the back basement of the stationhouse. Sergeant Murphy showed a newfound respect for him and allowed him a "look-see" at the evidence from the burning-body incident.

In a plastic bag were three items: a knockoff Pierre Cardin belt, an imitation Rolex watch, a Help-Wanted clipping from a Chinese newspaper.

There was a file of photographs, pictures of the torched body. The fake Rolex was on the victim's right wrist. *So he was left-handed,* Jack thought. A facial profile shot, side partial of left cheek and ear that hadn't burned off. A shot of the back and shoulder displaying a tattoo of the Chinese word *sot*, meaning murder.

On his feet, scuffed black Timberland boots, the *dirty boots* that the little girl's grandmother had described.

Jack scanned the chart. The corpse measured five-foot-nine. A hundred and sixty pounds. Under *Distinguishing Marks* the examiner noted:

1) Tattoo, left shoulder—Oriental word
2) Auricle Meatus Minor, left

Jack took the DNA tests upstairs, dug out *Gray's Anatomy* and found *Auricle, minor*, a stunted malformation of the cartilage that inhibits growth of the outer ear. Caused by hormonal imbalance.

Small ears. Ah Por's words pounded in his head as he pulled the rapist's file. Height and weight, the physical description was a match.

Small ears and fire.

Wielded knife with left hand.

The burning body. Jack knew the DNA from the body and the rape semen would prove to be identical. The rapist could run and hide, change his face even, but he couldn't escape the atoms and molecules in which he was grounded, the protein of his being, DNA, a tattoo he couldn't erase.

Jack took a breath, knew it still didn't matter. Even if they were identical, the courts didn't allow DNA evidence as the sole basis for conviction. If the toasted corpse was the rapist, then it was *Chinatown* justice that had found its mark. The rapes had ceased. In essence and in spirit the case was closed.

Red Pole

"No identification on body," Jack typed in his report on the California shootout. "Suspected Hip Ching associate."

No one stepped forward to declare the tall man missing. No one came to claim the corpse.

Jack ran the profile, but nothing turned up under Outstanding Warrants/Fugitives. The man was a Chinese John Doe when he was shipped back to New York. If the DNA blood match from Alexandra's handkerchief, and that of the Los Angeles motel shooter came back positive, Jack wasn't going to be surprised.

In Chinatown Golo's charity funeral went unannounced. He was cremated without ceremony at Wah Sang and consigned to a hole at the edge of Potter's Field.

Wood And Steel

The package arrived at the 0-Five courtesy of UPS and found its way to Jack's desk. He handled it carefully, suspicious, setting it down on a shelf in one of the open lockers while he considered. It was wrapped in plain brown paper, the kind old women used to play mahjong on. The return address was the top of a store receipt, *Asia Gifts, Inc.*, taped over the left corner. It bore a Chicago return address but a UPS barcode designated SF, for San Francisco. The numbers and letters of the precinct's address had been clipped from newsprint, and taped to the front.

Jack lifted the package and listened, then pulled his ear back, satisfied it wasn't a bomb. He sliced off the wrapping carefully, then slowly lifted back the flaps of the carton. Inside was a Chinese wooden box with a flat sliding drawer. A box within a box.

He pulled the drawer out gently, saw ivory first, then blued metal. It contained a lady's gun. In the back of the drawer was a tubular-steel silencer, and a folded piece of wrapping paper with Chinese words scrawled in black marker. When he unfolded it, he read, *The Big Uncle was killed by his driver, known as Wong Jai, plate #888.*

Jack lifted the Titan out with a pencil and ejected the clip. He knew Ballistics would work it for grooves, and Forensics for prints.

He wasn't expecting Mona's.

Paradise

The *Tropicali* set sail from Seattle on October 17th, bound for Maui. She was under Liberian registry, was six-hundred-sixty-feet long, could accommodate a thousand passengers and still cruise three days through the North Pacific at twenty knots. The *Tropicali* had four passenger decks, three swimming pools, two dancefloors, a stage, a discotheque, and eight bars. There was a shopping mall and a beauty shop called the South Seas Salon. The decks were named *Verandah, Empress, Riviera, Lido Promenade.*

Mona had booked a cabin on the Empress level, two decks above the Lido Promenade where the gambling casino and bar were located. She occupied a corner unit of the deck just above the stairwell to the beauty salon. Away from the masses, but close enough to the exits. On Empress, she was surrounded by a cruise group of Japanese office ladies. Good enough cover, she hoped.

Crossing the vast blue Pacific, she'd gotten rid of the black clothes, gone to the beauty salon and had her hair cut shorter in a mannish style, streaked it with amber. She wore dark red lipstick. At Maui she went ashore and bought hand-dyed silks and batik clothing, the better to blend into the cruise milieu. Except for the bursar, and the room attendant, no one would suspect she was traveling alone.

In Hilo she lounged alone on the Lido Patio deck, the ship having emptied, all other passengers having gone ashore. Lush rainforest beckoned in the distance, emerald gorges slashing into cliffs of black lava. White coral coastline against the weathered browns, reds, and blues of buildings. *Escape to paradise*, she mused.

Kona drifted past, beneath the heady aroma of ginger blossoms, blankets of sugarcane. Then Nawiliwili. Kauai faded into the panorama of Oahu, banana farms and pineapple plantations sweeping down almost to the sea. Exotic flowers in deep sculpted valleys thick with mango, pomelo, lychee trees. She pressed the jade ornament into her palm. *Changes*, the jade whispered, *changing*.

When the *Tropicali* docked in Honolulu, she visited the Kwan Yin Temple in Chinatown, her shape lost within the flowing Hawaiian shirt, her face hidden behind sunglasses under a floppy straw hat. She offered flowers and oranges, burned incense as she whispered a prayer for forgiveness.

Stone

Johnny sat opposite Jack in the interrogation room at Rikers. He stared straight ahead with vacant eyes and spoke with a dead man's voice.

"She said," he began, "the old bastard had found out about us, that he had put out a contract on me. I had to leave town right away. She was going to leave later, meet up with me in Los Angeles. She said she was expecting some deal to happen. We were going to be partners, do something outside Chinatown. Maybe go up to Vancouver. Something."

Jack pushed the microphone closer. "Speak up," he said.

Johnny smirked. "I took the bus, three days to Los Angeles. I found out they killed Gee Man near my car."

"*Who* killed Gee Man?"

"You know who."

"You mean the Hip Chings?"

Johnny nodded silently, glanced at Jack making a notation in his pad. He said, "It was meant for me, you know." He took a breath, then spat out the words. "'Stay at the Holiday Inn,' she said. 'Rent a car and come up north on Highway One.' She called me in L.A. and gave me directions. All along she set me up. Yeah, my prints are on the clip, but I didn't do the killing."

Jack watched him go distant.

"I just got her the gun. I showed her how it worked. I loaded it. That's how my prints got on it. And she set me up. She sent me running before the old man could get to me. The fuckin bitch. I'm innocent."

Gratitude

Captain Marino stood behind the big desk, said, "Way I see it, you went to San Francisco on your own time, while suspended. And brought back a dead illegal and the Uncle's killer."

He came around the desk.

"You got a box in the mail with the murder weapon inside. *Who* it's from, you don't know. And then there's the Uncle's girlfriend who got away."

He stood next to Jack now. "That sound right so far?"

Jack nodded into the Italian stare.

Captain Marino said, "Personally, I think you got a raw deal with Internal Affairs. I know, makes you wonder about being a cop. But for what it's worth, I think you did a good job." He shook his white-haired head. "Not easy being a cop these days."

Jack nodded again and left the big office, weighted down uneasily with the captain's gratitude.

Patience

It was almost eleven when the old men arrived quietly at the Hip Ching meeting hall, about the usual time of morning when they would normally be enjoying *dim sum*, snacks, and taking *yum cha*, tea, with the fragrance of oolong or chrysanthemum drifting above the round table in the back of the Joy Luck tea parlor.

The Hip Ching tong elders all knew about their leader's mistress, the one called Mona, the Hong Kong slut, the one they never mentioned for fear of causing him loss of face. Now they were faced with a dilemma. They'd discovered that money was missing, a hundred thousand dollars, from their benevolent community services account at the New Eastern Bank. It had been withdrawn, signed out in the Big Uncle's hand, four days before his untimely demise.

Now the loss of face was theirs. The free *congee* breakfast at the

Senior Citizen's Center they sponsored would be affected, and they would have to cut back the supply of Similac formula and flu shots to the Children's Health Clinic. There would be no more elaborate Chinese New Year's banquets.

Perhaps they could pay it off with money from other accounts, like the secret fund for free coffee and cakes at their daytime mahjong parlors? But quickly enough their words came back to the murder and the missing money. It had been all too clean and clever and they did not believe that the *see gay lo*, lowly car driver, was smart enough to have pulled it off. Not without help, anyway. Now they needed his help to find the mistress. Find *her*, find the money, and *wash* the whole affair. They needed to show the driver something, in good faith, for his cooperation, even from the small jail cell he was in.

San Francisco, after all, was just another Chinatown away, and with the Chinese world so small nowadays, how far could she have gotten? Not so far that their tentacles could not reach her.

Counselor

The white lawyer with the blue shark eyes and the easy suntan walked in wearing a Burberry raincoat, gripping a silver Haliburton briefcase like it was a fashion accessory. Captain Marino remembered him from past encounters. *Sheldon Littman, celebrity lawyer, who'd gotten an acquittal for master-of-the-universe broker Robert Cox, in the "rough-sex" killing of Jane Levsky.* Reasonable doubt was the name of his game.

"Shelly Littman," the captain said, deadpan. "That's impressive for a car jockey, Shelly. How can he afford an expensive suit like you?"

"Couldn't be the Hip Ching paying, could it?" asked Jack.

The lawyer dismissed Jack with a glance and a smirk. "*That*, gentlemen, is none of your business. I'm here to confirm his pretrial deposition testimony, taken by the Legal Aid lawyer, with the good detective here, and I'd appreciate it if you didn't cast aspersions on anyone who might be involved in this case."

"*Aspersions?*" chuckled the captain. "I like that, Shelly. I gotta get a new thesaurus. So, okay, we won't say bad things about the low-life player who got dragged in here for killing an old-time low-life bloodsucker." He gave Jack a wink. "He's all yours, counselor."

Littman coughed to clear his throat, then started. "Okay, Detective. You track my client all the way across the country, while you're on suspension, because some woman, *you* claim, called you on the phone and told you Mr. Wong's the killer, here he is, come and get him?"

"It wasn't that simple," Jack answered.

"Of course not, Detective, it never is, is it? Okay, and then, you receive, via UPS, from someone unknown, according to you, a weapon with an attachment of some kind, supposedly used to kill someone." He shook his head like he'd just recited a fairy tale to a three-year-old. Jack nodded in agreement. "And *why* does this "alleged informant" call *you?* Detective, do you have some *personal* interest in this case?"

"I'm interested in seeing justice done," Jack answered coldly.

"You see where I'm going with this, Detective? Even if the judge doesn't grant Mr. Wong bail, there's enough doubt here that no jury will convict him."

"Well, that remains to be seen. Johnny Wong's prints are on the murder weapon. At the very least, he's an accomplice."

"Yeah, *right*. See you in court." Littman left the captain's door open as he walked out, not bothering to look back.

Captain Mario said to Jack, "What do you think?"

Jack looked off into the distance. "The woman who took a pot shot at me in San Francisco? She's definitely involved. This guy, Johnny Wong, maybe he's dumb enough to be a fall guy, or maybe he's really in deep. But he's a flight risk, and no judge is going to grant him bail and let him walk, not with his prints on the piece."

His eyes focused, came back into the room and settled on the captain. "I'm willing to bet that the old men on Pell Street are paying for Littman because they're sniffing at something in the wind. They need Johnny's help to figure out what happened and they're buying time."

There was a brief silence. Then Jack said, "If Johnny's not the shooter, then it's the woman. Give the Hip Ching a couple of weeks and see what they turn up."

"What makes you think they can find out what you can't?" the captain asked.

"Chinatown doesn't end at Delancey Street, Captain. It stretches to Hong Kong, and Taiwan, and China. It reaches out to Chinese settlements everywhere. Sooner or later, there won't be enough space in the yellow world for a pretty Chinese woman to hide."

Marino frowned.

"At any rate," Jack finished, "Wong's arrest takes the pressure off us. And headquarters, too."

"Keep me posted," Marino said.

Jack went down the creaky stairs to the street. Night rain began to fall. He was off duty now and thirsty. He headed toward the Golden Star bar.

He'd talked a good game, but he was uneasy. He didn't see Johnny for the perpetrator, yet keeping him in custody was necessary. The longer he was incarcerated, the more pressure would build up. The longer it took to bring him to trial, the more time the Hip Ching would have to conduct their own investigation. If Mona was guilty, they had the best chance of scouring the world to find her. And then, eventually, the old men from Pell Street would produce evidence giving Johnny an alibi; witnesses would suddenly come forward with dated racetrack tickets, or cancelled passes to some Atlantic City concert featuring Hong Kong singers. They'd provide testimony as to Johnny's whereabouts at the crucial time that would be hard to disprove, that would be just believable enough to sway a jury, and the DA would decide to quash the indictment. The press was another matter, especially the Chinese press. While Johnny was in custody, the media feeding frenzy would abate. For the mainstream newspapers, the case would quickly fade, become just another seedy Chinatown killing. In the Chinese-language press, the left-wing journals would cheer for Johnny. The right-wing conservative papers would like Johnny lynched, but they would never mention Big Uncle's mistress. By the time the case resurfaced—with Littman for the defense playing for delay—Jack knew he'd be in a new precinct and out of the spotlight.

Finally, he reached the bar. The sounds of jukebox music spilled out of the door as he came through it, out of the cold rainy night.

Yellow Badge

At One Police Plaza the auditorium was packed with cop families, police cadets and veterans creating a proud field of deep NYPD blue. The Emerald Pipers band wailed, then applause punctuated the presentation of awards.

Jack stood on the stage in his neatly pressed blue uniform, before the mayor, the commissioner and an array of department brass, all applauding as the deputy chief pinned the Combat Cross above the gold badge over Jack's heart. It had taken him two shootouts to earn the little green-lacquered stripe with a cross in the middle, plus a promotion to Detective Third Grade, a step up in rank that carried a pay raise. The Internal Affairs investigation had been quashed.

When he looked out over the auditorium, Jack felt exhilarated yet sad. There was no family in the audience waiting for him.

He thought of Pa, and how proud he might have been. Maybe.

Black Widow

By Thanksgiving, *gwa foo* Widow Tam ceased to wear all black when she appeared in public, but kept the mask of grief on her face. At home, alone in the dark living room overlooking Chinatown, she wore her red embroidered nightgown every night to bed, her head nestling into downy pillows, wrapped in the blood color of new luck.

She felt thankful.

Her happiness had been completed when the police arrested Jun Yee Wong for her husband's murder and she received the Full Benefit, US $200,000, from Universal Life. Opening the windows, she felt the bite of frost tumbling out of the north, and began to think of sunny places where she could escape the New York City winter.

Bak Baan

Jack celebrated alone, chasing a line of boilermakers at the Golden Star. When he'd had enough, he returned to the park. He'd finally tracked down Ah Por to the free clinic at the Old Age Center. She was strapped to a gurney and connected to an intravenous line, dehydrated and delirious. The nurse said she'd been there almost a week and that, although the fever was breaking, nothing the old woman said made any sense.

Jack reached out from his alcoholic haze and placed the *bak baan*, mahjong tile, in her veiny clutch.

Ah Por rolled her eyes at him, called him *jai*, son, and passed the tile from palm to palm. She said what sounded to Jack like *panda sun, diamond sky, wind of salt water,* and began to tremble.

The nurse took the tile, returned it to Jack, and told him to leave as Ah Por lapsed into unconsciousness.

In the street, Jack repeated Ah Por's phrases but could not squeeze any clarity from them. He wandered down Mott Street, spinning from the boilermakers, clueless.

Pa

Sleep came in snatches of blinking REMs, fitful tiny periods of rest in a night of tossing and disconnected dreams.

When Jack awoke, he found himself on the floor in the daylight of Pa's apartment.

The sun was high and bright, unusual for a day in late October.

Sunlight streamed into the apartment, throwing thick slat-shadows across the floor, along the walls.

Family, he thought, *this is how it ends.*

He saw the Hennessy carton on top of the green vinyl uphol-stered chair, the only item of furniture still remaining. He crossed the empty room and took the mao-tai gourd out of the carton.

Sanitation had come for the mattress and the broken wooden chairs. The bed frame and boxspring were still good, and he had given them to the Old Age Center, along with the wok and the table lamp. The leftover clothes he'd taken to the Goodwill guys down on Houston near the Bowery. He'd given the rest of the books and magazines to the Chinatown History Project.

He took a deep drink, felt the heat as it went down. The super had taken out the garbage that Jack had piled into one corner. And that was that. The new family was moving in next week and they needed to get the place painted. Jack took the last hit from the gourd, surprised by its bittersweet taste, the sudden sticky ooze around the opening against his lips. He held the gourd upside down, watching as dark tarlike mud dripped out. He rubbed some of the sediment between his fingers, took a sniff. Opium, he realized instantly. No wonder he had had troubled memories, flashbacks with the photographs, been tormented by fragmented pieces of living left behind. Was it Pa's opium? Or had it been left on purpose for him? He'd never know, but wasn't sure that it mattered.

He set the gourd down.

Only the Hennessy carton was left. Fifty years of a man's life in a cardboard box. There were photographs, many of people Jack didn't recognize. Canceled bankbooks, a passport, eyeglasses, a flashlight. A black beaver fedora labeled Bianchi *icappelli di qualita.*

Jack was keeping all these, his memorabilia. There was the

porcelain Kwan Gung, an idol before which Jack could burn incense, bow, offer greetings, feel sorrow, hope. He'd miss Pa. Miss all the old ways he'd finally come to understand and respect.

Deeper in the box, a Social Security card, and Ma's Death Certificate, twenty years old. He tested the flashlight. It still worked.

He took the Hennessy carton and carried it out of the apartment. He carried it down the five flights of stairs, thinking how light it was, this box holding fifty years of living.

He stepped out into the bright sun and squinted down Mott Street. He paused for a long moment, let his eyes sweep over the streets, the neighborhood he'd grown up in, and was now leaving, yet again. Having been born into it, he'd been too close, and hadn't been able to see it clearly. Now, at long last, he did. Chinatown symbolized a bygone era, when the old Chinese bachelors were hemmed in by racist hate, denied their families, forced into doing women's work, to clean, to cook. The hate was still around, but the Chinese, no longer hemmed in, were free now to find their place in America.

Jack saw it clearly now: why Pa came—for opportunity, for himself, but more important, for his descendants, why he'd stayed until the day he died. And why all the tattered shreds of China that remained had been so dear to him. He'd lost so much of it that he couldn't bear to see it disappear from the single most important part of himself he had left, his only son. Jack had mistaken it for narrow-mindedness, but realized now it had been love.

Chinatown was a paradox, a Chinese puzzle he'd never been able to figure out.

Perhaps it's true, he thought, that one can never go back home, but then it was also true that a part of oneself always remains there, memories always with us in our hearts and minds.

The wind came up, blowing through his reverie.

So long, Pa, he was thinking, as he shifted the box up to his shoulder. He took a last look and made his way down the narrow winding street.

Lucky

It was early afternoon and the gambling basement was empty. Lucky went to the cheap card table by the rear wall and searched through the pile of newspapers stacked there. He was looking for news about Uncle Four's murder case, but found nothing except two tea-stained newspapers that were already weeks old. Lucky read the accounts in the *Post* and the *Daily News* and laughed. *How The Chinese Cop Broke The Big Uncle Murder.* And *Love Triangle In Chinatown Murder.* Jack, the hero cop.

Lucky toasted up some chiba and found an article in the *New China Times: Officials of the On Yee Merchants Association decried the recent violence in the community and proposed that civic leaders, tong leaders, and social workers cooperate with Fifth Precinct officers in a new Community Liaison arrangement designed to alleviate tensions between the various groups.* Lucky sucked in smoke, cracking a smile.

He had placed the blame for Gee Man's death on a renegade crew that had since been washed. In a generous gesture, he had called for a new peace between the Ghosts, the Dragons, and the Fuk Ching. Now he was the peacemaker. The new dealmaker on the block. The Merchants Association had nominated him to work with the police. The streets were profitable again. He went partners on a new gambling basement on Bayard Street.

He was looking forward to Christmas, when the next rush of gamblers would line his pockets. And when he hooked Jack and the other undercover *dogs*, he'd finally be truly untouchable.

Friends

Jack bought two packs of Red Rockets from the Lee Bao grocery, where fireworks were quietly available to the locals for ceremonial purposes. Now, thirty days after Pa's burial, Jack would be returning to the cemetery to set off the fireworks and to plant Flame Azalea bushes by his tombstone, *Rhododendron calendulaceum*, that would bloom full with red flowers in the spring.

The Lee Bao was on a small side street where Alexandra's grandparents had lived, and Jack thought about her as he made his way to the corner flower shop. He'd figured Alexandra wrong. Beneath her tough, pushy lawyer exterior, there was a woman who cared deeply for her people. He had called Alexandra about the handkerchief, and since her grandfather was buried at Evergreen, they had agreed to drive out there together that Sunday.

She brought the tins of roast pork and chicken, *bok tong go*, and packed them into the backseat of the Fury, next to the azaleas.

They visited her grandfather's plot first, where he lay under a foot-long grave marker in the old bachelors' section of the cemetery. They completed the ritual silently and then headed toward his father's grave.

The leaves were falling from the trees, dappling the landscape with swatches of amber, brown, and yellow. The sky was a crisp cool blue, stark sunlight shining, illuminating the autumn day.

They came to Pa's headstone. The ground was cold and hard,

and Jack had to force the folding shovel into the ground before he was able to turn enough dirt to plant the bushes.

They ran through the prescribed motions dutifully: Incense. Bowing. She braved the firecrackers.

They finished up with the *bok tong go* and the *cha siew* and bundled the incense and papers back into the car.

They had dinner by the bar at Tsunami, sake and beer, with sushi that floated by on a chain of wooden boats, new-tech Japanese style. When the distraction passed, Jack said soberly, "It's official. I'm transferring out. Two weeks vacation, then I report to the Ninth Precinct, in the Alphabets."

"Won't you miss the old neighborhood?" she asked.

"I'm not going far," he answered. "I'll still come by to eat and shop, but at least I won't spend every day in Chinatown."

"Feel bad?"

"I wish things could have worked out better. With what I knew, who I knew, I thought I could make a difference. But everything I do gets compromised. Makes me feel like I'm losing something."

She touched his hand. "This is your home."

"*Was* my home. I live in Brooklyn now."

Alex clinked her glass against his in a toast. "To home, wherever that may be."

"And where's home for you?" he asked.

"I've got folks in Hawaii. Oahu, where I grew up. You know, Waikiki Beach?"

"Sure." Jack grinned. "Paradise."

"I miss my family, sometimes, and the friends I left behind. The things we used to do when we were younger."

"Childhood in paradise," Jack toasted. They drained their sake cups.

* * *

"At all the family reunions there'd be a *luau,* with *poi* and roast pig, *mahi mahi,* and *maanapua.* There was sweet fruit and sunshine and we kids would just run wild."

Listening to her speak, Jack realized where he'd take his vacation time, before the transfer became reality, before the change of seasons.

Oahu, he thought, *downtime in paradise.* Recharge himself.

"This time of year," Alex was talking as if in a dream, "we'd visit the other islands, sell pineapples and macadamia sweets on board the cruse ships."

Jack could almost see it happening . . .

The local children clad in brightly colored *leis* and *pareos* performed the *hula halau,* dancing down the wooden Promenade Deck to the call of the *Hukilau* song.

Mona leaned back in a deck chair, relaxed in tan linen pants and canvas espadrilles. She loosened the silk scarf draped over her white T-shirt. The azure blue of the sheltering sky stretched as far as she could see. The ocean below was darker, sparkling and clear only when it rolled in over the reefs toward the white-sand shores. The caressing warmth of the sun had already put color back in her skin, and the rhythm of the ocean breaking against the bow soothed her, made her feel *ping on,* in harmony with the world. When she touched it, the jade sang, *Wind over water. Flowing. Auspicious omen to cross the great stream. Self-preservation. Water purges, revitalizes, but may bring chaos, danger. Weather the danger. Flow . . .*

She peered across the deck, saw the Chinaman's Hat in the distance, as the *Tropicali* made its idyllic journey past Oahu. A seascape of sailboats sliding through translucent green-blue water, whipped by wind.

She took a sip from the piña colada with the umbrella in it, adjusted her Vuarnets, and casually checked the straw Aloha bag on her lap. She saw the mahjong case containing the gold Pandas, the neat bundles of money, and the velvet pouch with the diamonds inside. After a moment, she put the drink down, and untied the Hermès scarf that had accompanied her from New York. She held it for a moment, letting it flutter in the wind, then released it, watching it sail free, disappearing into paradise.

In that moment she felt her soul set free, her body set free, from the oppression of men, of the world. She felt the tropical breeze through the gauze of the bandage on her thigh, the bullet wound healing, just a scab now. She knew the scars inside her might never heal, those memories were etched into her heart.

But here, and now, she was free, and nothing could force her back to that life again. She closed her fist over the jade, *holding earth under heaven*. Who could find her now?